AMONG THE WILD MULATTOS

AND OTHER TALES

Texas Review Press
Huntsville, Texas

FIRST EDITION

Requests for permission to acknowledge material from this work should be sent to:

Permissions
Texas Review Press
English Department
Sam Houston State University
Huntsville, TX 77341-2146

Acknowledgments

I owe a great debt to the editors of the journals who previously published some of these stories, often improving what I sent: Joe Killiany, Dave Housley, Richard Burgin, Rusty Barnes, Kim Chinquee, Mark Beggs, Shannon Gibney, Kathleen Alcala, Lindsay Stockton, and Vivian Shipley.

I also would be nowhere without the aid of many fine teachers: Robert McGovern, Ernest Lockridge, Randall Silvis, Jim Robison and Mary Robison. Special thanks to Lee K. Abbott, whose voice still stings and soothes every word I write.

For support and encouragement along the way, I'll thank George Singleton, William Giraldi, Steve Yarbrough, John Dufresne, Lewis Nordan, Sue Henderson, Brian Allen Carr, Dan Wickett and Matt Bell.

The following stories originally appeared in the below publications:

"The Hotel Joseph Conrad." *Jelly Bucket*
"A Public Service" *Booth* (online)
"The Finest Writers in the World Today." *Connecticut Review*
"The Lessons of Effacement." *Boulevard*
"The Story of My Novel, Three Piece Combo with Drink." [Published as "Three Piece Combo with Drink"] *Barrelhouse*
"Movie Star Entrances." *Night Train IV*
"The Most Famous Man in These United States." *Arkansas Literary Forum* (online)
"Ethnic Studies." *Indiana Review*
"Who Among Us Knows the Route to Heaven?" *Raven Chronicles*

Cover Design: Alban Fischer
Author Photograph: Tim Holbrook

Library of Congress Cataloging-in-Publication Data

Williams, Tom (Thomas S.), author.
  [Short stories. Selections]
  Among the wild mulattos and other tales / Tom Williams. ~ Edition: first.
    pages cm
  ISBN 978-1-68003-018-1 (p : alk. paper)
  1. Racially mixed people~United States~Fiction. I. Title.
  PS3623.I56634A6 2015
  813'.6~dc23
                              2015003444

For My Wife and Children

Contents

AMONG THE WILD MULATTOS AND OTHER TALES

The Story of My Novel,

Three-Piece Combo with Drink

During the post-lunch lull at Cousin Luther's, I thought I'd discovered the cure to all that ailed me.

I was staring at the menu of that fried chicken franchise in my hometown, trying to forget the three form rejection letters that had arrived that afternoon. Had the magazines been *The New Yorker*, *The Atlantic* and *Paris Review*, I'd have been on my way to the post office, but I'd been turned down by *Random Acts of Prose*, *Amateur Writers Unite!*, and an on-line number, *Boning the Muse*. With my fifty-first, -second and –third rejections of the year, behind me—and it was only mid-February—I might have preferred something stronger, but Muscadine was in a dry county and the package store fifteen miles away.

So I ordered a three-piece combo with drink and found a table in the back near the right hand window. I filled my cup with ice and Coke, then sat, my back to the counter and open kitchen. I ate my sides first, the silken slaw and peerless dirty rice, and was simultaneously anticipating the first bite of chicken. Still, glimpses of the Xeroxed slips—none bigger than a matchbook—flickered on the edges of my mental vision, which initialized a chain of recalled rejections: from editors and agents, writing programs and conferences, for grants and fellowships. So bad had things gotten in my four-year apprenticeship, I feared *Poets and Writers* would turn down my subscription request. And though I'd made no guarantees, I believe now I stood near a resolve: I'd write one more piece of fiction and send it out. If it came back, I'd quit right then and learn to content myself as the night manager of the Delta Lanes Bowling Alley.

But at Cousin Luther's, it was time for the chicken. Not time to eat it yet—I needed a few more steps before I'd savor this fried chicken, mass-produced but still as fine as any southern granny's. I spread two napkins on my lap, splashed on my tray a sizeable puddle of Louisiana Hot Sauce, and sprinkled the Cajun spice packet over my breast, wing and leg. I tugged my chair closer, made sure I was the only patron—a person of color, I tend to be wary about public consumption of watermelon, barbecue and fried chicken. And though it was perhaps my fiftieth visit to this particular Cousin Luther's that year, I parted my lips as reverently as any choir member about to sing a hymn, then sank my teeth into the chicken leg's flesh.

It was heavenly, I tell you. As good as my first bite had been years before. Better even, as it was hotter and spicier than I'd expected. My eyes blinked. Tears slid down my nose. I wanted to thank Cousin Luther (though he was a cartoon black man in a chef's outfit who resembled my Uncle Dobbs) and whichever of the high school dropouts in a hairnet had overseen the pressure frying. This was no mere piece of poultry! After dunking it in my hot sauce puddle, I took two more bites of the leg, all the while moving toward a state of mind that, looking back, I don't know if I'm glad I entered. At the moment, though, I couldn't have been steered from my present line of thinking, for as I tasted the chicken again and found it as good if not better than it had been earlier, I was thinking that something needed to be done to record this moment. Some action should commence that praised indefinitely how fine this three-piece combo with drink was. Still the only patron, I turned to the cashiers and cooks, as glum a crew of black and white youth that public schools and minimum wage could produce. They needed to know their greatness. They needed praise, but of a deathless sort, to remind them that appreciation existed for their culinary achievements.

A work of art would show them, I concluded. And naturally my mind turned toward a story. After all, I told myself, brass plaques tarnish, sculptures crumble, paint fades. Prose fiction endures. Yet who was I to think I could write that story? Weren't there three pieces of evidence to cancel me out as the one who might capture in a word or a thousand the splendid essence of Cousin Luther's Fried Chicken? Then a new thought occurred to me. While my general idea was strong, the form was off. A story would be too brief. This three-piece combo with drink needed a novel to commemorate it. Perhaps that had been my proper form all along? Hadn't the editor of *Scouting Life*, in my one personal rejection note, told me my autobiographical tale of racial strife in a Mid-south scout troop had the pace of a "longer work?"

Everything sounded so good, the impression of the task already having been completed overtook me. I sucked any remaining taste off the legbone and my fingers, certain fate had brought me here for this moment of realization. And while it may seem in my rendering that minutes had passed, this moment lasted only seconds, no more than ten and possibly fewer than five. I'd encountered no obstacles, though a pair hovered near: time and money. Did I have the patience and endurance to labor alone at this task? No agent had ever responded positively to any query I'd written about my proposed novels of biracial young men raised in the Mid-south; thus, an advance was out of the question. I knew, as I cracked the drumette from the wing and began to munch on it, that I'd need at least three months, without the bowling alley's distractions, to fully concentrate on this undertaking. Would it be three hundred pages? Four? How could I support myself? How would I buy more three-piece combos with drink! I didn't have enough in my savings, couldn't pawn my stereo and TV and sell my car and earn enough to pay rent, even at the cheapest of apartments. Help is what I needed, but no friend or family member would support me. All of them, my parents, my cousins, even Trina, my last girlfriend, had advised me at least once to give up my dream of seeing my smiling face on a book jacket. What to do? What to do?

My face was now slick with sweat and tears. After stripping meat from the wing with my teeth, I mopped my forehead with some napkins, closed my eyes and turned to the breast. Trying to savor the goodness—it was still sublime—I slowed down my chewing, and in so doing prompted the most exciting of thoughts: I could get a patron. And who better than Cousin Luther himself? Instantly, I saw myself standing next to Luther, both of us loose-limbed cartoons with bulging eyes, only my skin was two shades lighter. In his commercials, Cousin Luther often leapt up and clicked his heels, while spouting such jive as, "So spicy it'll make your lips quiver," and "You gon like it, else my name ain't Cousin Luther!" But in my vision he handed me a check the size of those given golfers and tennis players after winning championships. Then, as my mental cartoon continued, he uttered the restaurant's motto: "Go on and get you a good un at Cousin Luther's."

Later, I told no one of this vision, as I feared some might conclude a hallucinatory combination of spices and hot sauce had manifested it. All I can say, though, is that I was soon placing the clean bones from the breast on my plate and hurrying toward the counter. The cashier I'd ordered from, a blinking, brown-skinned boy with prominent teeth and a skimpy mustache, welcomed me again to Cousin Luther's, apparently having forgotten my earlier order. "I've already had a delicious meal," I said. "But I need to speak to the person in charge. I've got the most wonderful idea."

Blinking, he looked left and right as if unsure how to answer. He held up one long finger and said, "Wait a minute." Then: "Cassie? Mr. Bartlett here?"

A dark-skinned girl with braids beneath her paper cap stuck her head out from the drive-thru station. "In his office," she said.

"Follow me," the cashier said, and he came out to my side of the counter, leading me down a corridor past the restrooms to a door marked Private. He knocked. "Mr. Bartlett," he drawled. "Customer here to see you."

A colossal sigh could be heard. "Send them in," came a voice. The cashier blinked, opened the door, then left. Behind a sloppy desk sat a heavy-set white man with a crewcut, his short-sleeved shirt stretched tight across his chest and upper arms, a striped blue tie loosened but still strained by his massive neck. "What they do now?" he said. "Was it frozen in the middle? The rice hard? Whatever it is, you can either get your money back now and our apologies for the inconvenience or a certificate for two free entrees under five dollars on your next visit." He banged open a drawer and rummaged within.

I said, "It's not that at all." I seated myself. "I've got this idea that you have to hear."

Slowly, the manager sat back in his chair and closed the drawer. "You ain't here to complain?"

"Not in the least. I'm here to praise you and your staff, as well as the entire corporation. You serve the most fantastic chicken! But what if you had a work of art, a novel, to show the world how lucky we are to have such chicken? And sides! Do you have a minute?"

Warily, Mr. Bartlett drew nearer and nodded. Or his neck spasmed. Either way, I was telling him my plans and how I hoped for the financial support of Cousin Luther's, Inc.—a nominal sum, peanuts when one considered the potential revenue. He sat there, blinking as much as the cashier, and remained silent as I, with a rush of breath, said, "Don't you think that would be a great idea? For everyone involved?"

His mouth opened, but for a long time he didn't speak. Then, as I licked my lips—still sumptuous with grease—to renew my reasons, he said, "You'll have to talk to corporate. I can't help you."

"How do I get in touch with them?" I said.

He banged open the top drawer again. "Here," he said, thrusting at me an envelope with the address of their Little Rock headquarters. "I'm just the manager of 262," he said. "I can't help you."

In my reverie I hadn't expected a lukewarm response from anyone. In my reverie I was communicating with a cartoon spokesperson. But I didn't let Mr. Bartlett cool the heat of my resolution. I ignored his snort and derisive call of "Good luck." I went home and wrote immediately to the corporate offices, laying out in clear terms my proposal. As I figured on three months as the time I'd need for a draft, I requested five grand as an advance, roughly three months of salary from the bowling alley. What was that to them? I'd given Cousin Luther's that much money on my own! As well, I asked them to consider the attention they'd get if they subsidized me. My novel would serve as a permanent reminder to all of the greatness of their chicken—and their sides! How much did they spend on commercials? And how long before the public tired of the thirty second spots, requiring a need to produce newer and more expensive ones? In my last paragraph, I advanced a notion, which is the only part of the letter worth quoting: "If, as I am most certain, the product of our relationship is fruitful, might not others follow Cousin Luther's lead? And will not that put your fine corporation in the vanguard, remembered as the fried chicken restaurant that brought literature to the masses?"

After printing it out and signing it, I stuffed the letter into the envelope given me by Mr. Bartlett, then took it to the post office to assure it was headed to Little Rock in the morning. Anticipation swelled with me—as it always did when I mailed a submission—but this time I felt no fear. Not once during the first twenty-four hours did I believe my idea would fail. But soon, despite my confidence, the only thing to do was wait.

In the interim, I went back to shelving balls and spraying shoes with disinfectant at Delta Lanes. A story I'd forgotten about arrived from a magazine that claimed they no longer read unsolicited submissions. I wouldn't let that setback alter my enthusiasm. I wanted to write, but wouldn't let myself yet, not with so much of my hope hinged to the acceptance of my terms by the Cousin Luther's corporate office. I suppose I'd made up my mind then that if they said no, I'd no longer trouble the world with my fiction. But nothing could dissuade me from my belief in the project and myself. While I saved material and jotted down the occasional note, I grew more confident. Two weeks passed, then a third, while I clung to the writer's hope that the more time passes without word, the greater the chances success will result.

One thing about the novel I knew for certain was that it would be called *Three-Piece Combo with Drink*. On napkins and newspaper margins, I wrote this down, along with my name, as I'd read James Baldwin had while working on *Go Tell it on the Mountain*. A few times I ate three-piece combos at Cousin Luther's. Though I waved, no one working there recognized me. Daily, I ran to check the mail, often fantasizing whether the enclosed check required the corporate office to send their acceptance by UPS or Fed Ex. Occasionally, my confidence slipped, but not often or with enough force to change my mood. I spoke to no one about my plans, as friends and family had heard me describe previous stories and responded with either "Huh?" or "Why don't you just give that up?" Better to let them hear the good news, I decided, with the rest of the reading public—when the book was on the stands.

Then the day came when my mailbox contained more than circulars, bills and donation requests from my alma mater, Arkansas State. I saw the envelope, cream-colored and with Cousin Luther's smiling face on the left-hand corner. How many times had I stood poised like this? In the first year of my apprenticeship, I didn't know that when your SASE was returned you'd been rejected. Still later, I deluded myself into thinking that this time, an editor had used my SASE to deliver good news. But for now, as I tugged it from the box, I couldn't tell by the weight of the envelope what the corporate office had enclosed. Nor was I ready to open it outside. Had the news been negative, I don't think I would have made it back to my apartment. Yet I couldn't move. I suppose giddy anticipation finally stepped aside and fear, its shadowy companion, entered the scene. You've been delusional, I heard a voice say. Foolish. Wasting your time and that of a publicly traded company, one with far more important matters to consider. That some office lackey had taken the time to open my envelope seemed gift enough. A part of me hoped some coupons might be included with the kind but firm refusal.

But the sun was suddenly bright in my eyes and the mid-March temperature too high to stand there waiting. I went inside, cleared the card table I used as a writing desk and laid the envelope down, seam side up. I wanted a ceremonial letter opener but had only a butter knife. I considered a brief prayer, wondering if God loved writers so much He'd change the contents of an envelope if they promised enough contributions to charity. Then I recalled He hadn't transformed any rejection slips during the hundred other times I invoked His favor. Finally, after several false starts and a shaky glass of water that dripped on the envelope's top, I opened it. The letterhead featured Cousin Luther's head too, with a cartoon bubble leaking from his lips and reading, "Go on and get you a good un!" But the presence of a letter meant nothing. It elevated my heart rate, but then I remembered its author, unlike the editor of a journal, didn't receive two hundred queries a month, and didn't need to dismiss anyone with slips of paper containing reproduced regrets.

I pressed the top of the page against the table and unfolded the middle third, whereupon I could see it had been addressed to me and had obviously been typed by a human being. The characters had all left a slight impression in the paper, of a thick stock I had once used for cover letters, hoping to impress. I pushed down the bottom third, closed my eyes, prayed a little—"Dear God, just, just . . . ." Then I closed my eyes, let out a breath, and read.

Having no experience in getting an acceptance, and little versed with the prose of Public Relations then, I didn't know straight away what the letter meant. Only when I saw "Contracts should arrive—if you want to work with us—by courier as soon as we have verbal confirmation of your agreement," did I know I could retrieve my pens and pads. One might think I'd be overjoyed, dialing old girlfriends and English instructors who'd given me C's in order to taunt them. Surely a round trip to the county line package store was in order. But as I reread the letter, assuring myself Ms. Linda Parker was telling me Cousin Luther's Inc. had, indeed, "found irresistible your idea and is earnestly looking forward to the final product," I behaved as if the corporate board was watching me in my living room and I didn't want to betray my inexperience. Some might think my failure to celebrate signaled a fear I would actually have to now continue my cockamamie scheme. Nothing could be further from the truth. I called Mr. Dudley, my boss, to tell him I was quitting, then phoned the corporate offices and agreed to their terms. By the time I fell asleep at two a.m., I had written the first two chapters and was already dreaming of the third.

In truth, of all the time periods making up the story of my novel, this next was best. I wrote as one denied a pen for years, which is what I hoped to accomplish by forestalling any writing while I waited to hear from Cousin Luther's. When the couriers arrived with the contracts—three days after I received the letter—I'd reached chapter six, some seventy-five pages of, if I may be so bold, my best writing ever. And while I didn't get the five thousand I'd requested, I got three, and two surprises: a laminated card ensuring me a year's worth of free meals (under eight dollars) from any Cousin Luther's in the continental United States, along with the guarantee that *Three-Piece Combo with Drink* would be published. In my early consideration of the project, I believed Cousin Luther's representatives would send out the book to publishers when it was ready, yet I learned that, at their expense, Cousin Luther's was going to design, print, promote and distribute the copies. Some might have balked at this arrangement. A fried chicken restaurant's imprint is not the same as Knopf's or Simon & Schuster's, but this method of publication didn't bother me. In fact, the guarantee helped me write more swiftly. All along I'd known this would be a union of art and commerce, and I hoped that as much good as I might do Cousin Luther's, benefits would come to me, as well. And if the book was successful, I thought, who knew? Perhaps there'd be a sequel? Perhaps McDonald's or Taco Bell might demand my services? Or, once they'd finally made it to the light, my talents would gain the attention of traditional publishers and agents, and I'd be on my way to a career.

As I was writing, though, none of these vain thoughts littered my mental landscape. A reason for the ease with which I composed—twelve pages a day on average— was that my material was autobiographical. I made my first person narrator biracial—as I had with every other piece I'd written—though I moved his residence to Little Rock, which seemed a more appropriate setting for his occupation, sculpting. Never did I think too long about making him a writer: that seemed corny, too self-reflexive. Besides, I didn't want my audience to think my creation and I were that much alike and that his story was mine, though the plot possessed some parallels with my writing career. My character, Will, was more successful than I, but at the novel's opening, he'd reached a period of creative dissatisfaction. No longer able to summon inspiration, he longed for a return to the days when he hacked away at stone and shaped the figures his imagination commanded. I gave Will a love interest—though I was two years since my last date with Trina—to serve as a subplot: Will they marry? And Constance, whom I named for her enduring patience, wanted him to give up his aesthetic pretensions and become more of a commercial artist.

None of the obstacles I strew before Will hindered me in the drafting. Whenever my energy flagged, I'd reread the letter, especially the paragraph that concluded, "Your creative proposal assures us this novel is in the hands of an imaginative and skilled writer." Occasional daydreams befell me: I'd see myself dressed in a light-colored linen suit, before me an audience of adulatory readers. But I didn't, from my receipt of the letter to my delivery of the first draft, three months to the day later, take off one day from writing. Vain as this may sound, I was writing so well I couldn't wait to read the previous day's work, where I'd often startle myself with the incomparable prose and dramatic plot moves. When, for instance, in chapter four, when Will eats his third three-piece combo with drink and realizes that this fried chicken—and sides!—should be the subject of his next piece, I knew all along I'd write that scene, but little did I know how well it would come out. I never would have guessed I'd write the line that ended that scene: "It was all very clear—the key to the lock in my mind had appeared in the form of a chicken wing." At that moment I set down the pen and left my apartment. I knew I could do no better.

And when I finished the draft and typed it into Microsoft Word—five marathon sessions of eighteen-hour days—I felt a slight sense of remorse. I knew I'd see the characters again—there were first draft details I was fuzzy on. Where did one purchase marble? Was marble even used by sculptors anymore? Even still, I felt, as I drove to Little Rock in my temperamental Ford Escort to hand over the draft to Linda Parker, that I was letting go my offspring, and that now I had the difficult task of sharing it with the world. I knew Cousin Luther's would be happy. In the three hundred and twenty pages, I mentioned the restaurant two hundred and nine times, Will and Constance ate there in six scenes, while Will ate there alone in five more. Four scenes featured him in his studio, eating chicken as he worked on his masterpiece— titled, like my novel, *Three-Piece Combo with Drink*. And with the climatic scene, where Will donates his sculpture to the corporate headquarters (a place I'd never been and hoped to visit for second draft corrections), I determined that they had a book they couldn't have made better themselves.

My meeting with Linda Parker confirmed these feelings. In her airy, third floor office (I'm made my version of the headquarters building too gray), she paged through my manuscript, remarking again and again on her pleasure. An intense and thin woman with odd glasses, she was not an Arkansan but a Chicagoan whose hard midwestern nasality startled me. "Oh, that's perfect," she said one moment. Then: "Exactly what we wanted." She looked up from the pages on her lap and eyed me over the bridge of her glasses. "We haven't wasted a penny on you."

Before I headed back to Muscadine, Linda described to me the rest of the process while we ate three-piece combos with drink in celebration, and then she posed me next to a cardboard cut out of Cousin Luther for a publicity photo. There'd be a review of the manuscript by her PR staff, who'd suggest changes, then they'd approve my changes and pass the draft to the legal department, who'd make sure there were no libelous passages (I had, in fact, made a few derogatory comments about KFC). Then, definitely before August, the book would be out, and she and I would work tirelessly to promote it. When I stood outside the entrance to the building, ready to drive home, Linda shook my hand. Her grip was stronger than mine, and she wished me well. "Just wait," she said. "This is the beginning of a wonderful partnership." I wanted to hear more, but I'd already taken up two hours of her time and another meeting was calling her away. But I had praise enough for the drive home. I could follow in my imagination the sequence of certain successes. Probably more than at any time, after those impossible years of what looked like failure from all directions, after, at last count, three hundred and forty seven rejections, along with dozens of manuscripts that were lost and dozens more that returned unread, after all that, I believed I was a writer.

But no matter how ebullient I felt, it was the end of the period of creation. As soon as I put my pages in Linda Parker's hands, a new phase commenced. And when I got from her a call two weeks later that she was sending the corrected copy, I felt a pain in my chest. I'd expected changes. I'd even done some research on sculptors in the interim. Still, I'd unconsciously hoped my typed draft was immaculate, ready to go directly to bookstores. As well, I was anxious to get the book released, as I was almost out of money. My taste for Cousin Luther's chicken hadn't ebbed—and they had a new catfish platter worth at least a short story—but I used my free meal card there less and less.

Once I calmed down, I grew confident again. "Of course there were changes," I said to Linda. "Can't wait to see them."

"You did all the hard work," she said. "All we did was refine it."

"Thanks," I said.

"So let's get this puppy out in the world! All right! In time for late summer reading!"

Her excitement restored my confidence even more. When she hung up, I nearly ran to the mailbox. But I had another day at least to wait.

I tried not to predict what had been done with my draft in the hours I waited, but I couldn't quit thinking about the alterations. Essentially, I expected refinements, as Linda had suggested. A more accurate description of the corporate building. Perhaps some pruning of descriptive passages and a tightening of scenes. I wondered whom I'd be working with. Linda or another PR person? Though stubbornly some resistance remained, I looked forward to the experience of working with an editor. To be truthful, I was also hoping for someone who wouldn't mind hearing some of my ideas for future work.

The corrected draft arrived two days after Linda's call.

There is a moment in many stories like the story of my novel where the artist finds himself the victim of unscrupulous managers, promoters and executives but has no recourse. The contract he signed assures his hands are tied. This innocuous phrase tripped me up: "Cousin Luther's Incorporated assumes the full production of this work." I doubt any of Muscadine's personal-injury attorneys could have read that phrase and known Cousin Luther's intent. Even had I been warned, I wouldn't have done anything differently, as I believed this was the only way to see my book into print.

The title was the same, as was Will's ethnicity. (Linda told me: "He taps into both white and black demos.") And they kept him a Little Rock sculptor who donated his work in the end to the corporate office, though the point of view was switched to third-person, a new crisis was added to the plot, and his medium changed to metal, which ensured a lot of noisy welding with flying sparks. Otherwise, *Three-Piece Combo with Drink* was unrecognizable. They'd made Will the manager of a Cousin Luther's on the west side of town who sculpted in his free time. And, unlike a real manager, he actually ate the food prepared at his restaurant, at least once a day, often while commenting, "Damn, this is fine fried chicken! The best!" Constance was dropped, as a fiancée got in the way of Will's many demonstrations of virility (including a scene in which slaw and two biscuits serve as a means of arousal). Moreover, their Will needed far more energy than mine to fight off thinly disguised fast-food competitors, who schemed to acquire secret recipes and sent into Will's restaurant hordes of street brawlers, Ninjas, snipers and finally a twenty foot robot with laser beam eyes. The structure—a series of violent set pieces with bed-hopping and chicken eating transitions—was execrable. The language, absurd. And anyone with an IQ over sixty would have sensed that no one who ate as much fried chicken as Will would have "arms of steel, legs of iron, and abs you could grate Cousin Luther's Chunky Fries with." The complete and utter badness of it would have made me laugh hysterically had the book not had my name on it.

I could have refused. I could have returned the money to buy back my draft and done with it what I wanted, taken out all the overtly commercial references and let it stand on its own as a novel of art, love and fried chicken. But I may as well be plain in this account: I didn't know if I'd ever get this close again. I hoped this would be a foot in the door, so to speak. Not everyone writes *Catch-22* or *Invisible Man* the first time out! This was, let's say, my *Typee*, my *Fanshawe*. The next one—and I was convinced I'd write another—would make everyone forget *Three-Piece Combo with Drink*. At least that's what I told myself at the time.

As for what happened after I signed off on all the changes, and Linda Parker said, "Awright," like one of Al Capone's henchmen, I wish I could forget. I wish I could forget the garish cover of a shirtless Will with a drumstick between his teeth, clinging to the robot's neck (whose wrecked robot corpse would become the raw material for Will's final sculpture). I wish I could forget the author photo—the very same one of me and the cutout of Cousin Luther, where it's difficult to tell who's more lifelike. I wish I could claim that all this was endured by another, but sadly I know all too well it was me.

A tour followed, with book signings and readings, but I didn't set foot in a Border's, Brentano's, Square Books or That Bookstore in Blytheville. Instead, in Memphis, Jackson, Hattiesburg, Fort Smith, Dallas, Monroe, St. Louis, and tiny truck stop towns in between, I sat near the heat of open kitchens, signing grease-spattered copies, shook hands with my audience (most of them quite charming, if illiterate), posed for photos with more cardboard cutouts of Cousin Luther, read chapter excerpts over the hiss of the deep fryer and the squawk of the drive-thru speakers. As a courtesy, most managers suspended counter orders, though there was that angry manager in Grenada, Mississippi, a fellow mulatto who shouted he had too many orders to fill.

At every stop during those four months, I got reports from Linda Parker, so many that I started taking Benadryl before bed to muffle her blunt vowels echoing in my head. Cousin Luther's was doing quite well with the novel's release, bolstering its reputation among its existing clientele, luring literary types and earning praise from state and local agencies for promoting literacy. As I'd predicted, other chains tried to duplicate the success, the national ones chasing after King, Chrichton and Grisham, though no deals were ever made after my royalty arrangement—the sole mistake Cousin Luther's made as first time publishers—was learned. If a nobody like me was getting twenty-five percent, many reasoned, the costs for an author of note would certainly eat most of the potential profit.

Meanwhile, I was growing wealthy, selling more and more books, appearing on regional morning radio and TV shows. On one such appearance in Shreveport, the young Latina hostess asked me to read her "favorite passage"—a section where Will, in my estimation, cruelly victimizes a female spy from the KFC clone, General Sandy's Tennessee Fowl. I stumbled over the words and got lost twice, causing Ms. Rivas to say, "It sounds like you haven't read that aloud before." Though this might have been the time to loudly proclaim the truth, I surprised myself with an awful equivocation: "Sometimes, when you're writing a book, it's as if someone else takes over." Then, before I forgot, I uttered what I was contractually obligated to say: "Go on, *read* you a good un at Cousin Luther's."

By the end of the tour, I looked horrible: bloated from so much fried chicken and sides, hollow eyed from lack of sleep, my normally fawn color veering toward a jaundiced yellow. I showered five times a day but couldn't remove from my nostrils the stench of fried food. The linen suit I'd bought to match my dream was stained, sloppy and unable to hold a crease. I was tired, felt older than my thirty-four years, but had one last appearance, a special one in Muscadine, "home of my inspiration," according to Linda Parker. It was to be a huge occasion: all my friends and family—the harshest critics of my desire to write—promised to be there, as would be representatives from the press and Cousin Luther's, the mayor of Muscadine and the town council, along with Mr. Dudley, my former co-workers at Delta Lanes and many bowlers who once rented shoes from me. After my limo ride to Franchise #262, I tried to smile and hoped only half of the people would want to buy me a three -piece combo "because you like them so much." Everyone greeted me at the door, Linda Parker leading the way. She grabbed me by the sleeve and, in the crush, accidentally scraped the side of my head with her glasses. Flashbulbs popped and sizzled, seemingly disembodied fists held aloft copies of the book. My parents were elbowed out of the way by Trina, my ex, whose last words to me had been, "I should never get involved with mixed nuts."

Then #262's manager, Mr. Bartlett, resplendent in a short-sleeved shirt and a tie as wide as a napkin, pulled my other arm and shouted, "I'm glad to have been the one who helped this writer achieve his goals." Even the kitchen crew and cashiers applauded then, all with a new paperback copy of my novel in reach.

Automatically, I did my act: read from the first and ninth chapters, answered a few questions, then signed books. My high school grammar teacher, Mrs. Ball, was thrilled I'd mastered the comma splice, and Uncle Dobbs—looking grayer than Cousin Luther but still nearly his double—wanted to know if the girl Will beds on page one-thirty-seven was modeled after Danita Strickland, a former Miss Black Muscadine. Then, after posing for more photos and choking down more three-piece combos with drink, I found an opportunity to escape. Everyone who'd ever known me was skirmishing to be interviewed by the just arrived TV crew from Memphis, trying to say it was he or she who'd been the one who helped me out the most. I said my piece to the reporter then excused myself to the bathroom. While no one was looking, I ducked out the door. Almost immediately, I stopped the driver of a Ford F-150 and he agreed to take me to my apartment, as it was on his way home. Once inside his cab, though, I saw skittering on the top of his dashboard a copy of *Three-Piece Combo with Drink*. The driver, an older white man with a John Deere cap, squinted at me, then we both looked at the book. He spat out the window, wiped his mouth and said, "Ain't you that fellow?"

Even in my beleaguered state, I was too quick for him. Shaking my head, I said, "I get that all the time."

One pleasure of living in Arkansas is the many regions where a person can easily hide. With my money from the book—and there was a lot of it; I can't complain about that, save to say Cousin Luther's got even more, especially after they sold the movie rights—I was able to rent this cabin in the Ozarks. I'm so far from the nearest dirt road that the only person who knows I'm here is my landlord, who doesn't have my real name and has only seen me with the beard I've grown to go along with my ball cap and dark glasses.

I came here not just to avoid the celebrity brought on by my novel. I wanted the self that authored *Three-Piece Combo with Drink* to disappear so a new one could emerge and write the fiction I want to be remembered for—instead of a novel whose greatest virtue is the two-for-one three-piece combo with drink coupon on the back page. My *Moby Dick* and *Scarlet Letter*, if you will. If I publish anything else, it will have to be under a pseudonym—an idea that came too late for the first book. Sadly, though, any identity I construct will face the same difficulties I encountered when laboring without success for so long. No wonder in the sixteen months I've lived here, I've not produced one page of fiction. Most days it is impossible to squeeze out a sentence. I started writing this very account with the hope I might stumble onto a new idea, but imagination comes harder and harder, as if by forgetting who I once was as a writer, I lost all connection to whatever talents I once had. Above all, I hoped a sober setting down of that which occurred with *Three-Piece Combo with Drink* might once and for all silence the voice that seeks to continue in the vein of that book. But as I write these lines, a phantom taste spreads across my tongue, and even though the closest Cousin Luther's is miles away, I can sense the direction I need to take to get there.

A Public Service

Our work is necessary. Don't let our detractors sway you. They're prudes or privacy hounds or pornographers. It's best not to fraternize with them. Besides, name me an enterprise that doesn't conjure up controversy, I'll show you something as lifeless as a Jehovah's Witness's birthday party. Don't stop now, buddy. We need you to stay committed.

I'm not saying our work is easy. Certainly, the size of today's video recording device has made it easier for a solitary man to saunter through the shopping plazas and outlet malls of America without getting caught by those he might be recording. But it's not easy to locate the kind of woman our subscribers want to see and, almost simultaneously, direct and power on the device so that it might capture her assets. You know Merrell? From Memphis? Like you, he started with the eye for the job. Especially liked pears. Still shoots more of them than any other kind. But in his early weeks he'd only *report* to us the number of large and lovely ladies he'd spotted. I'd show Ruland over there Merrell's emails and we'd conference call him. "Now get some video of them," we'd say. For a while, the only video he showed us was of the inside of his pocket or the ground just ahead of his feet. An occasional blur, with his raspy cough the soundtrack.

Of course, Merrell got better. You've got to get better, else you get out of the business. But soon enough, Merrell showed us and our subscribers some of the biggest butts of the Mid South. He's got a real talent for spotting whale's tails and plumbers' cracks, too. But that didn't come from just walking around. It came from discipline, practice, making sure you cut a hole in your jacket pocket and had the camera ready *before* a BBW crossed your path. I'm not saying you could become as good as Merrell, but you never know until you try, right?

Our work does come with danger, too. I won't deny that. Take Thomas, poor guy, in San Antonio. That part of Texas may be home to the most diverse and ample backsides of the United States, but the kind of fellows who like their women with a little size don't appreciate some gangly white guy lingering and leering while these ladies roll past. In a week, he got beat up by two Mexicans, two blacks, followed by a Vietnamese guy who was dating a mixed girl. Lost three teeth and enough blood to put him in the hospital, but Thomas got video of each of these girls. Great video. Ruland thinks the mixed girl must have been Black, Mexican and White. Said her booty was so big and Thomas's zoom so close you could see the strain on the seams of her jeans. Said he kept waiting for them to just open! Pop!

I'm not saying this to scare you, though. I'm trying to get you where you need to be, which is out there tracking down these chubby cuties. We get nearly two thousand hits a day and our advertisers couldn't be more happy with us. Our subscribers keep asking us for more footage of big girls' behinds. Plus, it's summer and there's no telling what kind of miniskirts and short shorts might be barely covering these wide loads.

Listen, I want you to do well. I want Rearview.com

to continue to do well, most of all, but I want you to be a part of it. We're like nobody else out there. What we do is real. What we capture, what our subscribers demand, is not some made up porno with stick figure girls, limp dicked guys and everybody on coke. We're out on the streets. Easley in Greenville just parks outside the Goodwill. Doesn't leave the parking lot. We're in the grocery stores. You can't go wrong in the ice cream and Lean Cuisine aisles. Hell, we're at the ball games. Hurwitz, over in Baltimore, gets great stuff hanging out near Camden Yards. We're out there were they are, those big, baby dolls.

Denigrating women. Invading their privacy. Who told you that shit? We're showing women, real women, single moms, widows, divorcees. Ruland and I, all our guys, we're making them look good. But we're respectful. We don't show faces so nobody knows just who it is who's carrying around all that sugar. We're celebrating these large ladies. We love these hefty honeys. We're practically a public service. Anybody who spends five minutes on the site could see that. Over ten thousand minutes of footage of the juiciest big booties on the internet. In, Ruland says, their natural habitat. Shaking behind a shopping cart. Bending over wide to tie a kid's shoe. Jiggling a little bit while the girl taps her foot at the bus stop. Classic stuff.

And we're just getting started. That's why I wanted to, you know, give you a boost. A pep talk. I like you, buddy. Ruland does too. But you want to worry about what these massive mamas are thinking, what their feelings are? Go work for the census. You want to travel, admire some wonderful scenery, make some cash while you're doing it, you stick around. Trust me. You'll get that next fat fanny in your frame and you'll think you were put on earth to do nothing else. Then you'll come back to me and Ruland. You'll be the one telling us just how necessary our work is.

Movie Star Entrances

The strip mall did not look promising. Especially brown and nondescript in a neighborhood of nondescript, brown strip malls, all but three of its storefronts were empty. The few domestic vehicles parked on the cracked asphalt stood near Space City News, an adult bookstore, while the specials advertised in the window of the discount luggage shop lead Curtis to believe its owners would soon be joining those who'd left this ignoble commercial space behind. But he was not here to leer at explicit videos or purchase a half-priced Samsonite. He'd endured the Katy Freeway on a Friday rush hour to get to 11525-C, whose dark windows he was presently trying unsuccessfully to peer through. Yet after the one-hour drive from his office at the museum, he needed to do more than stare. There was less than a week until the party, and he believed or hoped—after reading the ad in *Public News*—that the people at Movie Star Entrances might give him, at last, a reason to feel he was worth more than just a glance.

He tried the door, but the knob would not turn. Another reason to go home, Curtis thought, before noticing the intercom to his right. A TALK button sat below the mesh screen, but he took a moment before pressing it. It was early June and already his first Houston summer had his glasses slipping down his nose, while in his pockets he carried two wrinkled handkerchiefs: one for allergy-related sneezing, the other to mop his face and neck. Such ablutions, he sensed, would do little to make him more presentable. And because he was not sure what services or products were offered by the creators of that enigmatic ad, he didn't know if he should care how he looked. He took the paper out from his inner jacket pocket and read the postage-stamp sized ad again. "Want to Stand Out in a Crowd? Need a Personality Makeover? Try Movie Star Entrances," it read, surrounded on the back of the newspaper by ads for phone sex, escorts, penile enhancement, vasectomy reversal, and the truly desperate personals where the lonely and overlooked pleaded, as in one case, that "the handsome gent in the white tank and shorts at Heaven on Pacific thought too a moment had been shared Sunday the 10th." Curtis shook his head. He believed himself unlike those who paid for such personals or answered the other ads. This was different. He was different. But he needed to see if the people here could do for him what Sherry and Alonzo Jenkins, his white mother and black father, had not. He pressed the TALK button. After a feedback clogged snarl, he winced, then said, "I saw your ad?"

With a sudden buzzing noise, the door sprang open a space. Curtis stepped back, examined the door and remembered his flat thumb still holding down the TALK button. "Thank you," he said, let go, then slipped inside.

The lighting was either poor or deliberately obscuring, for Curtis had a difficult time navigating his way into the shop. Instinctively, his hands slapped at the air, and his fingers scraped the plywood walls that hemmed him in like a steer led to slaughter. After a few cautious steps, he'd reached a wider space, and his eyes had adjusted slightly. "Hello," he said, as tentatively as the first victim in a haunted house movie. He was about to say, "Is there anybody home," when two people, a woman and a man, stepped before him and said as one, "Welcome to Movie Star Entrances."

"Hello," Curtis said, shrugging at this display of his vocabulary's limits.

"How can we help you?" the pair said again simultaneously.

"I saw your ad," Curtis repeated.

The woman stepped forward, her face closer to his than Curtis liked, so he stepped back. She was nearly as tall as the six foot two Curtis, and her long face was plain and pale but topped off exotically by a leopard print hat that resembled a cross between a Shriner's fez and a skier's toboggan. A measuring tape curled over her shoulders and earrings in the shape of Academy Awards dangled from both lobes. "What's your jacket size?" she said. "Forty? Forty-two?" In a second, the measuring tape was off her neck, and she stretched it across his shoulders and down to his wrist in snapping motions.

"Always a good start, measurements," the man said. Shorter than his partner and Curtis by a good six inches, he was now circling Curtis from the front. He smelled of a cologne Curtis could not recognize, he relying primarily on the perfumes of Right Guard or Mennen Speed Stick. "Where did you see the ad, if I might ask," the man said. "The *Press* or *Public News?*"

As the woman moved in to measure his inseam, Curtis thought about his answer, preferring to set a favorable impression. The *Press*, a far more reputable free weekly than the *News*, featured color photography, responsible journalism, and was available at grocery stores and legitimate booksellers. The *Public News* had ink that bled on your finger tips, its writers tossed off one screed after the other, and was most likely found at newsstands that carried racing forms, cheap cigars, and swinger magazines. "The *Press*," Curtis said, while both strangers circled him, the woman holding both hands before her face, her thumb tips touching, creating a wide channel to look through. "We haven't advertised in the *Press* yet," the man said, grinning. "I'm sorry, but that was a little joke. No one admits to reading the *Public News*, it seems."

"I'm sure our customer misspoke, Ramon. Isn't that right, sir?"

"Yes," Curtis said, blinking. "I misspoke." With the dim lighting and this odd pair circling him like hyenas, he felt disoriented. His right hand clutched both handkerchiefs in his pocket, while his left touched the leather of his wallet to make sure it was still there. "Tell me," he said, then cleared his throat. "What is it you exactly sell here?"

This stopped the pair. The woman's large hands fell to her sides, while the man, Ramon, said, "Drama. Flair. A sense of mystery and intrigue. Tell him, Miriam."

"Do you mind?" the woman said.

Curtis looked at her. A long cigarillo dangled from her lips. He nodded then watched as her black-painted thumbnail coaxed flame from a matchhead. Grandly, she inhaled, while Curtis tried to remember other Miriams he knew, landing only upon his maternal aunt, a schoolteacher from Omaha who never married. Now that smoke was expelled from her lungs, making Curtis blink, this Miriam said, "Dean in *East of Eden*. Or *Rebel*. Leigh in *Gone With the Wind*. Taylor in *Suddenly Last Summer*. Orson Welles in *The Third Man*." She paused, smoke streaming from her fingers. "I could go on."

Curtis knew all the names but had only seen one of the movies, *Rebel Without a Cause*, and that on TV when he was seven. He couldn't recall a line or a scene and was about to ask for clarity, when Ramon stepped next to Miriam, took her free hand in his as if to dance, then said, "You see those faces fill up the screen and you cannot look away."

"It's the Movie Star Entrance," Miriam said.

Ramon, touching the back of one hand to his forehead, pretended to swoon. Cigarillo between her lips, Miriam stepped behind him to catch his fall.

The strange need to applaud brought Curtis's hands together, as he believed a performance of some kind had ended. As well, he wondered if the time for his exit had not just arrived. Still, the museum staff party loomed like a promise and a threat, and he hadn't gotten any nearer to a plan for how he might display himself there, nor had he learned precisely what this odd, melodramatic pair might do for him. "Um," he said. "I'm still a little unsure what it is you do."

"Ramon," Miriam said, nodding. In a practiced glide, the little man moved toward a wall, snapped on a light switch. Instantly, the room was flooded with brightness that hurt Curtis's eyes but slowly revealed that before him stood row upon row of costumes. Movie posters covered the walls and props were gathered in all corners. Fascinated and spurred on to run his fingers through the various materials or feel the heft of the Styrofoam boulders or try on the rubber Godzilla suit, Curtis could also detect that Miriam had moved closer and was still examining him. "My," she said. "If I didn't know better, I'd say we couldn't do much for you. The light confirms it. Ramon."

Ramon returned to her side. For the first time in Curtis's viewing, the small man stayed still, and Curtis could now see how heavy he was, despite the loose fit of his pleated slacks and silk shirt. His smooth, plump chin rode the golden scarf wound around his neck and his mustache was trimmed to the width of a pencil line. His hair, swept up and gelled, shaped a pompadour as perfect as a toupee. "You're absolutely right," he said. "Posture needs work, as ever, but bone structure, the eyes. If you don't mind me saying, sir, just what is it you want us to do for you that a merciful deity already hasn't?"

Never one to take a compliment well—especially one regarding his looks—Curtis ducked his head and wiped his chin against his shoulder. He wanted to thank Ramon and Miriam, yet remembered that, in a way, this was why he was here. All his life he'd been the only one, the only person in Des Moines with a black father and white mother, and it seemed since kindergarten he was telling someone each day why he had blue eyes or why his tan didn't fade or whether his hair was naturally curly. Though the answers always led him back to his parents, the attention he received caused Curtis to see himself as a rather special individual. Even though he displayed no discernible talents or gifts, on the basis of being singular, he believed he'd attained a loftier space in which to travel. Yet it also urged in him a desire to find a place where his presence was not so spectacular, where he might be among others like him. When he learned of the open position at the Museum of Fine Arts, he thought Houston might be that place, and when he was informed he'd gotten the job, it seemed the first of many opportunities to establish his place among the elite. But, from his arrival, among his coworkers and in the city itself, he sensed, for the first time, inferiority. Betty Huynh, an assistant curator of sculpture, could tell of a childhood of deprivation in Vietnam, along with harrowing accounts of escape and travel in rickety boats operated by unscrupulous pirates across the Pacific. These were rivaled by the stories of Manuel Olivares and Olga Trevino in preservation, who with their families, from El Salvador and Chiapas respectively, traveled on foot to a wide Rio Grande monitored twenty-four/seven by the Border Patrol and coyotes who smuggled folk across in a panel truck for a price. Even Stephon Garnett, the security supervisor, told tales of survival and narrow escape that made the Third Ward of Houston sound as precarious as any Third World nation. As well, these folk, and more, were all handsome, intelligent and cosmopolitan, while Curtis began to see himself as just a biracial suburbanite from the Hawkeye State. Who'd accrued no honors at his second-tier state college and distinguished himself very little in any field. Yes, he worked at one of the finest art museums in the nation, but in accounting, a job he feared some software designer was preparing to render obsolete. All he had was the story of his parents, how they met, and everyone at the museum had already heard a similar tale from Teresa Peters, a beautiful biracial woman who'd been working as assistant curator of design in the two years before Curtis arrived. And as her parents had met in Africa, when her white father was in Soweto on a Peace Corps mission, her story was far more compelling than Curtis's account of his parents bumping fenders in the parking lot of a Moline shopping center. Now, as he winced at this thought, he could also sense that either Miriam or Ramon was about to ask him about his ethnicity, but first he had to ask them, "What is it you actually do with all this stuff?"

Miriam and Ramon regarded each other, their eyes affectionate, but not, it seemed to Curtis, for each other. Tapping ash on the cement floor, Miriam said, "We make it possible for the most ordinary person to be extraordinary."

"But how?" Curtis said. He looked down to see both hands twisting a handkerchief, as if he could not hear soon enough what they might do for him.

After a sweeping gesture with both hands, Ramon said, "With all this and some training. Along with a few little technical treats."

"Don't forget movie star magic," Miriam said. "Tell us, sir, what's your name?"

"Curtis Jenkins."

"So, Mr. Jenkins," Miriam said, grinding her cigarillo

on the floor with the thick sole of her black shoe. "What kind of impression do you want to make? Bold? Subdued? Enigmatic?"

"I just want to stand out in a crowd, like your ad says."

"What's the occasion?" Ramon said.

"Office party."

Ramon's fleshy hands smacked together. "Wonderful," he said. "We're perfect for parties."

Though he couldn't see her, Miriam was studying him again, Curtis believed. He turned to his left, spotted her pointed chin resting on the back of her long hand. Go ahead and ask, Curtis was thinking. And she did: "Jenkins," she said. "That's what, an English name?"

Curtis didn't want to play at guessing, so he volunteered, "I'm biracial. Mom's white, dad's black."

"Really," Miriam said, her inquisitive eyes roaming his face like the fingers of the blind.

"Thought I was picking up a little Creole vibe," Ramon said, snapping his fingers to a tune only he could hear.

"Well, then," Miriam said, "That gives us something we can build on."

"You should see some of the dreck that comes in here," Ramon said, conspiratorially.

"Shhh," Miriam said. "We want you to know, Mr. Jenkins, that your secret stays with us."

"None will be the wiser," Ramon said. "We're very discreet."

"Now about price," Miriam said.

"Yes." Curtis touched his wallet in his pocket and was about to take it out when he realized he still couldn't say—in ten words or a thousand—just what services they performed here. "But you still haven't told me," he began.

Miriam pointed a finger at him like a gun. "You'll be very pleased. I promise."

"All our customers are. Would you like to see some of our testimonials?' Ramon turned toward a small desk in the back, cluttered with sequins and feathers, with a tailor's dummy seated on the folding chair beside it. Above hung a garishly colored poster for the original *Cape Fear.* Curtis blinked, then shook his head. "Just tell me what you're going to do for me."

"First, Ramon and I will need to confer," Miriam said. "We know your situation, have gotten a pretty good look at you. I've got some ideas, and I'm sure Ramon has some too, but we'll come up with a variety of packages. Costume, training, music. The works. It'll be your choice."

"Music?"

"Fiber optic speakers," Ramon said. "The latest technology."

"But we're not cheap," Miriam said, crossing her arms. "Not for all that we do.' She nodded gravely toward Ramon, who closed his eyes and dipped his chin into the folds of his scarf.

"How much?"

"Five hundred," the pair said as one.

Again, Curtis blinked. He dabbed his handkerchief at his nose and said, "You take credit cards, yes?"

"Of course," Miriam said. "Every one, including Diner's Club, for a touch of swank."

"So what happens next?"

"As I said, Ramon and I will confer, then get back to you in a week and a half."

Curtis stepped forward to grab one of them. "I don't have a week and a half."

"Oooh," Miriam said, tsk-tsking like a schoolteacher. "Our shortest turnaround has been eight days."

"We could do it in five," Ramon said. "But the training won't be as effective, not with so little time. I'm afraid you won't get your money's worth, Mr. Jenkins."

"I just don't have that much time," Curtis said, as if repeating his claim would somehow alter their position. But it was all he had. He walked forward another step, handkerchief streaming from his hand.

"You realize you won't get our finest," Miriam said.

"What if we knock off ten percent?" Ramon said. He beamed, suddenly fell to his knees, his dimpled fingers clutching each other. "Please, Miriam, for Mr. Jenkins?"

"All right," Miriam said, patting Ramon on the head. Then she strode down an aisle between rows of costumes and stopped at the cluttered desk in the back. She blew sequins off a desk calendar. "When is your party?"

"Week from tomorrow," Curtis said, pushing his way past the costumes on both sides, their hangers clinking together. Miriam pulled a pen from beneath her hat, then straightened it on her head. "We'll have to see you here on Wednesday." She shook her head. "That's so little time for preparation."

Ramon jumped between them, clutching the loose material of his shirt near his heart. "But we must, my dear. We must for Mr. Jenkins!"

Curtis looked at the floor. Back home and at school, gays were as common as biracial people, yet here in Houston—in his neighborhood, his workplace, the checkout lane at Kroger's—he'd become almost immune to their ubiquity. Still, rare was it that he witnessed such a campy act as Ramon's. He felt enthused and embarrassed, as if he was seeing something he shouldn't. Yet when he looked up, he saw Ramon kissing Miriam on the lips. He had to stand on his toes and she had to dip her face toward his, but their mouths were open and the kiss lasted so long that Curtis stared hard at the desk calendar, noting how each block was massed with notes and names. He wasn't their only customer, of that he was sure, which assured him he wasn't throwing away his money. Then he heard Miriam say, "Ok, we're agreed. You need to meet us here, at this time, on Wednesday. And we'll give you the fifty dollar discount."

"Don't tell anyone," Ramon said in a stage whisper. He handed Curtis a sheet of paper, on top of which was written in a flowing calligraphic hand, "Testimonials." Then he wiped his mouth with his sleeve.

"Here," Miriam said. Between her extended fingers was a business card. Curtis reached out his damp palm and she set it there. "In case you need to call us."

"I can still say no, right? If I'm not happy with any of your packages?"

"Oh yes," Ramon said. "But no one ever has." With that, he donned a silk magician's hat from the rack and made a tossing gesture toward the cement floor. After a thunderous crack, a thin, acrid plume of smoke rose between Curtis and Ramon and Miriam, not enough to obscure them, but enough to assure Curtis it was time to depart.

While he waited for Wednesday, Curtis worried over the likelihood that this might work. At his apartment in the Heights, he tried to replay the events of that curious Friday evening but always felt unable to reconstruct it all, as if the smoke from Miriam's cigarillo or Ramon's trick had insinuated itself into his memory, obscuring key moments that might make sense of it all. He rented the films they'd spoken of, watching them for the entrances of the stars, save for the *Third Man*, which bored him to the point that when Orson Welles is uncovered by a kitten, Curtis was getting a beer out of the fridge. None of the films gave him a better sense of what might happen at the party, as Curtis believed the secret behind all these magnetic entrances was simple: the actors were beautiful people, whose faces and frames would attract attention in any venue. How would that help him in a room full of people far more handsome than he? What could Ramon and Miriam possibly do with his long, narrow face, his one eye noticeably lower than the other, his mouth that hung open at inopportune times, his blackhead studded nose? There was, however, consolation in the testimonials that Ramon had given him to read. Each customer avowed complete satisfaction, relying on such empty but seemingly important phrases as "awesome," "fantastic," "spectacular," to describe the impact this pair had on them. Of course, they could have been fictional, manufactured by the showy Ramon, yet as Curtis's eyes would pass over some of the more in depth paragraphs of praise, he'd feel they were genuine. One in particular, from Mr. Ed. D of Tomball, read: "My friends and family got to see the person I am in my own thoughts and dreams. Plus every day feels like a new day. Each time I walk into a room, I remember your advice on presentation. Even in sweatpants and t-shirts, I know how to make a Movie Star Entrance!" Curtis didn't believe anyone could fabricate that kind of reply. Besides, he told himself, he had to trust Miriam and Ramon. They appeared to be his last and best hope.

His mornings and afternoons at the office confirmed to him how important an opportunity the party was. Everyone was talking about it. Interns and curators and security guards were planning on bringing their significant others and staying until the hotel-keepers kicked them out. With all the employees from the museum in the Sheraton ballroom, Curtis expected it would look like the floor of the UN. And without the magic Miriam and Ramon had promised, he would be so very overlooked. He might as well stay home, or just break his lease and find a job in the Hawkeye State, where he doubted he'd even be the only biracial man anymore.

One afternoon, he sat at his desk, turning Miriam and Ramon's business card over with his thumb and forefinger. It was not a flashy card but elegant and understated, with a simple font and a rich tan color, only a shade lighter than Curtis. He was debating whether to call them when he noticed that the back read, "Miriam and Ramon Guererro, Proprietors." He stopped turning the card. They couldn't possibly be in the same family, unless one was adopted, and then there was that kiss he witnessed. But married? Those two? He didn't know what to make of that. The effort of his concern must have shown on his face, as Teresa Peters strolled by and said, "Keeping you busy, huh?"

Curtis looked up, clapped the card on his desk. Not only had Teresa arrived first and blunted the impact of his story, she was gorgeous: tall, but not thin like Miriam, with green eyes and wavy, brown hair that flowed like water on her head. Intelligent, too. A graduate of Brown, member of Mensa, she oversaw a book club in which no one, Curtis heard, was allowed to draw comparisons between his or her life and that of the central character. He now looked up at Teresa, who was tucking her hair behind her ears. She smelled of jasmine perhaps, and something else, an elusive scent he'd have to ask her about. But Curtis had forgotten precisely what she asked him so he nodded and shrugged simultaneously. After she left, waving, he looked at the card, then his desk calendar, willing the days to pass.

Wednesday night, at Movie Star Entrances, Miriam and Ramon both appeared excited to see Curtis. After he'd been buzzed in, he saw them waiting at the end of the narrow entryway. They linked their arms with his, then led him to the costume and prop area, murmuring about how much they'd looked forward to this day. Curtis was disheveled as the last time, perhaps even more so, as the AC in his Taurus had been floundering. When they three reached the stark light of the costume area, Curtis blew his nose and saw a three-way mirror that hadn't been there before. "Now we can begin," Miriam said. Dressed in a cheerleader's sweater and short wool skirt, a leather jacket and combat boots, Miriam lit a cigarillo. Her hair, a startling platinum, couldn't have been longer than a quarter of an inch. Curtis's wet lips parted, while Miriam grabbed the back of his neck with her thin fingers and forced him to regard his face in the mirror. "Are you ready to be a star?"

Curtis could see his head nodding, manipulated less by his own thoughts and more by Miriam's unexpected strength.

"We were up all night after you left," Ramon said, the top of his head just below the height of Curtis's chin. "Saturday, we argued. Good thing we had other clients to occupy our attention."

"Indeed," Miriam said. Her grip relaxed but her fingers still cradled Curtis's neck. "But the time constraints gave us inspiration, I think."

"Because," Ramon said. "Sunday morning, over huevos rancheros at La Mexicana, we just looked at each other and we knew. We really knew."

"What do you want first?" Miriam said, finally letting Curtis go. "Music? Clothes? Posture and movement lessons?"

"We've got a lot to do in not much time," Ramon said.

In the mirror, Curtis saw his mouth still agape. There were so many things he wanted to say, but he couldn't get his lips working. He blinked and looked at Ramon's reflection. The little man appeared ready for a golf outing in 1930, with liver and white spectator shoes, high socks pulled up to his knees, baggy knickers and an argyle sweater over his tan long sleeved shirt. A bowtie, undone, hung around his collar. His hair was slicked back on his head and, surprisingly, his carefully trimmed mustache was gone. "I, I, I," Curtis stammered. "Clothes, I guess."

"The dressing room awaits," Ramon said and pointed toward a tall folding screen, from which a garment bag hung. Steered in that direction by Miriam, Curtis's feet were dragging, as if to keep him from nearing some inevitable and foul fate. He was feeling that these two weren't just odd, but perhaps deranged: they wanted him unclothed and vulnerable. Yet a vision—as real as anything else in the room—of Teresa Peters's face flickered before him, her smile widening as if she'd seen something that pleased her. He pulled the garment bag from the screen, quietly determining the screen's width and height would keep him sufficiently guarded from prying eyes, then stepped behind. A folding chair stood there, and he laid the garment bag on it. He stepped out of his shoes, peeled off his pants and rearranged his bunched and damp underwear. Ramon, near but clearly on the other side of the screen, announced, "You see, I went with my gut. Still, Miriam insisted you had the look of the dandy about you."

"Uh-huh," Curtis said, taking off his necktie.

"Oh, open it up. I can't wait," Ramon said.

Curtis unzipped the bag. In it was a majestic seersucker suit, an item Curtis had never dreamed of owning, yet his fingers, as on their own, smoothed their way down the lapels.

"I hope that's reverent silence," Ramon said.

"Shh," Miriam said. "Let's give Mr. Jenkins some time to himself."

Curtis owned three suits, two purchased in a package deal at an outlet store in Des Moines, one a graduation gift from his parents. Grey, black and blue they were, and made, he believed now, as he stepped into the seersucker pants, out of some material approaching burlap. He slipped on the jacket and was hastily pulling his fists through the sleeves when he saw yet another item, no longer obscured by the dazzling suit: a white shirt with a forward point collar and French cuffs. With both arms in the sleeves of the jacket, he didn't want to take it off, even for as lovely a shirt as it was. "I'll try the shirt when I get home," he said.

"As you like, Mr. Jenkins," Miriam said.

Curtis stepped from behind the screen. Ramon ambled over, cradled his arm again in Curtis's, directing him toward the mirror and saying, "You'll recall, I said Creole. And I stuck with my guns. It's a bit of a compromise, I think, between old New Orleans and your general dandy. Especially with these two items." In one of his pudgy hands was a red, paisley pocket square, which he fitted into Curtis's coat pocket. With the other hand, he snapped the bowtie from around his neck and presented it to Curtis like a blindfold offered to a prisoner facing the firing squad. "Sir," he said.

"Ever owned one before?' Miriam said, her combat boots and motorcycle jacket creaking.

"No," Curtis said, feeling ashamed for the moment, as if he should have owned at least a dozen.

Ramon huffed, then busily fussed with the red material. In seconds he had a bow as well as a loop to slip over Curtis's head. "Look in the mirror," he said. Curtis heeded the command and saw, in the three mirrored panels, a figure he only faintly recognized. All the flaws of his face—his mismatched eyes, his spotty nose—seemed distant or overshadowed by the splendid cut and fit of the suit. He looked to the inner pocket to see the maker, then saw stitched there, "Movie Star Entrances." Had one of these two made it? Suddenly, Ramon's face was next to his in the mirror. Curtis looked down to see the stool on which Ramon's spectator shoes were resting. "A few adjustments," he said, tugging the ends of the tie. "And so there's no pressure, this one comes with an escape hatch." Curtis felt Ramon's fingers slide beneath his collar and then Ramon pulled both halves of the tie apart and put them in Curtis's hand. "What happened to your mustache?" Curtis said.

"Oh," Ramon said, touching his upper lip. "Why? Do you want one?"

Curtis shook his head, fitting the tie together by its hook and clasp, then putting it under his collar again. As his eyes took in the sight of himself, they drifted down to the desultory sight of his black-socked feet. He was about to mention this when Miriam came up on his left, holding two pairs of shoes in her mannish hands. "White or dirty?" she said.

"It is after Memorial Day, so white is acceptable," Ramon said, hopping off his stool.

"But," Miriam said, placing the shoes on the floor on both sides of Curtis's feet. "White is more problematic if there's going to be food and drink. Spills, you know."

"As I said before, he can keep a chalk bag in his pocket for touch ups."

"But his pockets will be filled with the remote control for the music."

"You're right," Ramon said, suddenly smiling. "The music. Do you know this one, Mr. Jenkins?"

Kneeling, Curtis looked up at Ramon. During their brief squabble, he'd decided on the dirty bucks, and now watched as Ramon pointed a remote toward their desk. Rollicking piano chords spilled from the speakers. Curtis could see in his imagination long dark fingers trailing up and down a keyboard. "'Tipitina,'" Ramon said.

"Professor Longhair," Miriam said, scraping her thumbnail across another matchhead and lighting a new cigarillo.

"But . . ." Curtis said, looking at Miriam, then back to the shoes. How did they know what size he wore?

How could he make this music play at the party? "How does," he began.

"Just leave it to the experts, Mr. Jenkins," Miriam said, pointing her finger to herself, and then to him.

By the time Curtis left Movie Star Entrances, it was ten past midnight. No one was entering or exiting the adult bookstore, but the nearby roadways were busy and the Houston air still felt thick and viscous as it entered his lungs. The garment bag, containing his new shirt, a pair of cufflinks in the shape of dice, his old shoes and pants, lay across his back, as he carried it with his fingers locked around the sturdy hooks of the two hangers. Silently, he was counting one-two between each step, making sure that the rubber heels of his bucks hit the ground first, so as to lend a sense of what Ramon called "heedless frivolity" in his gait. Before Curtis could leave, Ramon commanded that he keep up this step, his spine as straight as a soldier's, for at least a twenty count. And Ramon marked out each second by snapping a riding crop against the side of his baggy knickers, shouting in deliberate syllables, "You are not in a rush, Mr. Jenkins. How can I see you if you are speeding by?"

Now, as he made his way to the car, Curtis believed he was improving, both in pace and posture. He still needed to count but was starting to feel he might be able to walk this way with little effort by Saturday. However, he was unsure he'd fully trust the sound system they'd equipped him with, which consisted of a small cassette player in his inner pocket and two undiscoverable speakers beneath the points of his shirt collar. The wires connecting the player to the speakers were sewn into the seersucker suit. In the right pocket lay the remote control. No one, Miriam promised, would detect a bulky outline on him, and they'd hear, without quite knowing the source, the magical piano of Professor Longhair, whose music Curtis had never heard a note of before this evening. Curtis clicked the remote control button and could hear the music but distantly, as if listening to a Walkman without headphones. He clicked it off. Neither Miriam nor Ramon would explain to him precisely how everything worked, though Ramon did concede it was, "Very James Bond." Then he said, "Shhh," behind a chubby index finger while Miriam wreathed their eyes with more cigarillo smoke.

Now, as Curtis got into his Taurus, he attempted to be careful, which is why they'd made him leave in the outfit for the party. He'd wanted to change back into the clothes he'd arrived in, but they both assured him that he needed to get familiar with the suit and shoes and pocket square and tie. (Ramon tried but could not convince him to try on a straw boater.) He had to adjust his ordinary actions to keep the suit and shoes free of the stains and scuffs one picked up every day, never knowing of them until the clothes were taken off. Further, Miriam said he had to feel his presence in the suit, had to let the movie star within emerge. Only then would Curtis Jenkins truly make an entrance on par with those of Dean, Taylor and Welles. After laying the garment bag on the passenger seat, he brushed off the driver's seat, then gently lowered himself, careful to lift his trouser cuffs well above the grime and squashed coffee cups on the floor, keeping his sleeves distant from the dusty dash. He started the car and the first breath of his AC reminded him of its failings on the way over. Yet he overlooked this possible malfunction, as he was very near believing that whatever this was—a charade or masquerade—he would not regret his outlay of four hundred and fifty. He backed out of the parking lot and drove home quickly, so he might get in bed and dream.

*   *   *

On the evening of the party, for some time Curtis did not want to enter the hotel ballroom. Ramon had warned him of this, labeling it opening night jitters and counseling that he bring along a flask to provide him some quick courage. But Curtis feared he'd be shaking too much to drink without spilling. What had happened to all the confidence that carried him through Thursday and Friday? He'd raced home those nights to don the suit, then promenade—that was his word—around the perimeter of his living room, believing every moment that he was about to commence a journey that would take him in a direction so far from where he'd started that, even if he wanted to return to the old Curtis, he'd be too distant to see the route there. So far, this overly warm and muggy Saturday evening—the afternoon had seen the season's first hundred-degree reading—he'd only managed to make it from his car to the lobby's men's room, and he sneaked there through a side entrance. He wasn't ready to leave the shadows of the stall farthest from the entrance, and fortunately few had used the rest room in the forty-five minutes he'd been hiding, trying to summon the swagger and ease he'd had earlier this morning when he practiced his strolling saunter in his underwear. Ok, he told himself, when he at last stepped out of the stall. Just take a look at yourself, you're fine.

In the mirror, he knew within five seconds that something was missing. He checked everything once more, patted down his lapel, secured the knot of his bow tie, stamped away any light dust that had settled on his shoes. Still, he could not keep from seeing the reflection of Curtis Jenkins wearing a nice suit. Before, he'd seen a different person entirely, one who didn't count his steps, who didn't worry about spilling barbecue sauce on his shirt, who didn't toy with his cufflinks every minute or so, as if to advertise he wasn't used to wearing them. What he needed, he knew now, was Ramon and Miriam at his side, dressed however they chose on Saturdays—likely in a Valkyrie's breastplate and Zorro's cape and mask. It was through their eyes alone he confirmed all would be well. His own uneven pair could only detect fear while his mind predicted misfortune.

He thought he heard the door open and ducked back into the stall, waiting there until he heard another guest urinate, zip up, flush and exit. Curtis crept out again, and washed his hands, wishing already for a drink. Or a cigarillo of Miriam's, though he didn't smoke. Some prop he could hide behind deeper, something to completely obscure the person he believed himself to be since he moved to Houston: as ordinary as all those Iowans he'd left behind to find those among whom he thought he belonged. He then dried his hands with a handkerchief, which he promptly put in the wrong pocket, the right one that held the remote control. As if he'd touched an iron skillet on the stove, he pulled back his hand, pocketed the handkerchief, but allowed his fingers to find the button on the Zippo sized remote. The heavy beat of blood in his ears prevented him from hearing anything playing clearly. Yet he had to think it would work. Even if they weren't here beside him, he had to trust Miriam and Ramon. They were his hope. He silenced the music. It was seven o'clock.

At last, he pushed himself out of the restroom, counting one-two between steps, putting his weight on the heel and keeping one hand in his left coat pocket for balance. He stumbled a time or two, scuffed his soles against the tile floor, but kept moving until he reached the atrium of the hotel lobby. Well-lit, cool, and decorated by potted palms and plush furniture, it was attended by busy and helpful men and women in uniforms, and held many attractive and well-dressed guests, his peers, about to walk to Curtis's left and enter the ballroom. He could follow them or turn right and disappear into the deep Houston night. If he did that, though, Curtis felt he might as well go home and start packing then and there for a drive back to Des Moines. Yet he owed it to himself, to the now sizable balance on his Master Card, to at least try. He must. On his way to the double doors, above which hung a sign reading, the Palmetto Room, he stumbled, but then righted himself before falling and was certain no one had seen him.

Inside, the plan was to wait for a five count at least— "ten would be achingly sublime," Ramon claimed—and Curtis lingered for seven before he began his first circuit of the room. He was to take two, minimum, then stand by the bar and place his order for a drink, preferably a Pimm's Cup, if they had one. If not, a Planter's Punch or a sazerac. He was to remind himself that he was as suave as Cary Grant, debonair as Sidney Poitier, and as stable as Gary Cooper. And he tried, strolling around the room, almost forgetting the sound system, then clicking it on as soon as saw some co-workers, seated at nearby tables. Through his peripheral vision, he could see that virtually everyone was present. If nothing else, his earlier hesitation had provided him with a full audience, and he hastened to keep moving. Soon the gait he'd left Movie Star Entrances with had returned, and he believed heads, slowly but surely, were turning. Curiously, he wondered now if the boater might have been as perfect on him as Ramon believed, yet he would let nothing distract him as he started his second circuit.

This go around was slower, as Miriam had suggested. "Let them think they can approach you. Don't look at anyone yet. Speed up just as they're getting near," she said. His lips twitched as he fought to keep from smiling. He had to make it to the bar. The chatter around him did not diminish, and he could have sworn he heard his name a few times. Ahead, he could see the bar a few steps away, manned by two Anglos in white shirts and western vests. He slowed his pace even further, turned off the tape, made sure the bar was clean and dry—no damp rings or cigarette ashes to mar his sleeves—then leaned an elbow on the smooth, polished wood.

He was ready to order his drink when Deena Singh, a smallish woman with skin as dark as Curtis's and large oval shaped eyes, came up to him. She worked in painting preservation and had rarely spoken to Curtis, save for salutations in passing. "Curtis," she said tonight, her accent mostly British but her manner Texan. "What is that?" She touched his lapel in a way that made him think she was trying to tear it. But he allowed her the privilege, remembering that Miriam had warned him of peoples' needs to measure he who, upon entrance, simply does not seem real. "I'm drinking a Shiner Bock," Deena said, her eyes not straying from him. "What about you?"

For a second, Curtis thought he should join her, but he stayed with the script and ordered a Pimm's Cup. "A what?" Deena said, finally letting him go and looking away, but her eyes returned, just as the blonde bartender with the mustache said, "A little New Orleans, tonight?"

Curtis nodded.

By the time the drink arrived and Curtis had tasted its curious combination of gin, lemonade and Sprite, along with accepting the bartender's apology that they had no cucumbers, Deena had grabbed Olga Trevino by the wrist. Dressed like Deena in art-crowd black jeans, thrift-shop jacket and t-shirt—Olga's featured the Virgin de Guadeloupe playing drums behind a guitar-wielding Frito Bandito and a somber Cesar Chavez on bass—Olga reached out for Curtis's sleeve as Deena said, "Will you look at this guy?"

"I see," Olga said. "I saw!" She swept her other hand

through her inky black bangs and came so near Curtis could smell the liquor on her breath. "Curtis," she said, tilting back then leaning forward. "I just can't. Carla," she said, waving her hand toward Carla Armbruster, a matronly member of the foundation board, who'd met Curtis several times and on each occasion forgot the previous introduction. Tonight, though, she looked as though she was trying to memorize his features, and her lips parted slightly as she turned her silver head side to side. "Goodness," she said. "I wondered who the man in the seersucker was."

And so things went for Curtis much of that night. He hardly had the chance to speak as, one after the other, his coworkers passed him along like a talisman everyone hoped to touch for good luck. Betty Huynh posed with him for a photo her younger sister snapped. Felipe Rivas, the film series director, bought him two Pimm's Cups, and Mrs. Marion Lloyd, also of the foundation board, asked him if he'd gotten the suit from Harry Sidney, but Curtis couldn't respond, as her daughter, Miranda, a grad student at Rice and museum intern this summer, wanted to know his lunch schedule for the next week. Everyone who approached him possessed, in effect, the same manner, as if they all saw the same thing. They smiled as they drew near, then positioned their bodies and hands to keep him from getting away too soon. At times, he pressed the remote in his pocket to play a few rollicking bars, gleefully watching as faces around his looked to him, then away, asking their neighbors if they too heard something.

It was nearly quarter to eleven by the time he'd left the ballroom. Until then, Curtis had traveled only about thirty feet from the bar and said little more than hello and "It's the suit" to all the people who spoke to him. Had he been privileged to receive this kind and amount of attention of late, he might have grown bored by the monotony of it all—everyone praising essentially the same thing, voicing this comment: "No, it's more than just the suit. You look different tonight"—but as it had been so long since Curtis had experienced such consistent attention, he reveled in each repeated praise. Now, as he stood in the men's room—where only hours earlier he'd cowered—he took one last look in the mirror, seeing, if he squinted, a fair approximation of the gent perceived by all who'd been in the ballroom. The second he entered his apartment he would certainly type a testimonial for Miriam and Ramon, for he knew, without them, the triumph of this evening could not have occurred. Yet, as he dabbed his handkerchief at his forehead and neck, he wanted to have one more set of eyes range over him, one more voice of praise: those of Teresa Peters. If he got just a "Wow!" from her he'd count that as tacit admission that he and she were, at last, equals. And he'd feel certain that this night would be for him the beginning of a succession of like moments, and he'd never feel inferior again in his own tawny but undistinguished skin. If he had Teresa's approval, he'd need little else.

Finding Teresa, though, proved more difficult than he'd suspected, as many of the revelers were exiting the ballroom and he was moving against their flow. Some wanted to stop and comment, ask if he'd lost weight, if he'd been to Café Annie yet, if he'd been working out, if he had any thoughts about the Surrealist exhibition slated for next month. Curtis smiled at everyone who queried him, yet he kept moving, avoiding contact and grasping hands. After a few moments of struggle, he reached the ballroom, which now had the look of a less than festive space, with the chairs and tables pushed out of their orderly patterns, the lighting far less moody, empty bottles and upended cups spilling out of the full trash cans. But after a brief scan of the remaining folk, Curtis spotted Teresa, standing near the bar with Stephon

Garnett, both dressed in black, holding napkin-wrapped bottles of beer. After altering by a few degrees the angle of his approach, giving Teresa a full-face view, Curtis thought of turning on the tape, changed his mind, then made sure he was looking in every direction but hers, which resulted, as he'd hoped, in Teresa saying, "Curtis. Hey, Curtis. I thought that was you."

Curtis waited until she started waving before he looked at her. Then he arched his eyebrows in surprise and shook Stephon's hand vigorously before turning to Teresa and saying, "I didn't know you'd come."

"I did get here late," she said, pausing to sip from her beer. Stephon tilted his bottle back as well, and briefly Curtis felt regretful, staring at his empty hands and cursing the fact Teresa had missed his entrance. The bottle popped out of her mouth with a whispery sound, then Teresa said, "But I knew you were here."

"Heard about you right away," Stephon said. Taller than Curtis, Stephon was much darker-skinned, with a clean-shaven face and skull that emphasized the length of his narrow head. Ordinarily, Curtis saw the security supervisor as one who always outclassed him in dress and comportment. He especially smelled better. But tonight he felt Stephon's equal, as if Stephon had shrunk an inch or two, or Curtis had grown.

"Everyone's been saying you looked so different," Teresa said. Her nails, painted pink, flashed before him as she reached out to touch his sleeve. Inwardly, he flexed his shoulder muscles to keep from shivering. But it wasn't affection he wanted. He wasn't thinking he could date her. He just wanted to know she considered him her peer, an equal. After she let go his sleeve, as if just feeling the material, he awaited some other gesture, one that would confirm this. In a moment, he realized she and Stephon were talking, possibly about Curtis, but he wasn't listening. Of all the party-goers he'd been around tonight, these two were the most inscrutable: as he focused on their conversation, he could have sworn they were talking mostly about the suit. Not him. Then Stephon looked at his watch, a massive and shining Rolex that made Curtis glad he'd left his Seiko at home. "We better get going," Stephon said.

"Yeah," Teresa said, finishing her beer. "Don't want to turn into a pumpkin."

Nervously, Curtis laughed, then studied his nails, trying not to let his eyes or face reveal his disappointment. "Don't let them see the you you are," Miriam said before he left on Wednesday. "Give them the you they want to see." Despite this minor letdown, though, he'd still write a testimonial for them. Of that he was sure. Then Stephon put his hand on Curtis's shoulder and said, "Want to come along? We're headed to another party."

"After hours at Jamaica, Jamaica," Teresa said. "Should be wild, mon." Her hand rested on his other shoulder, her fingers squeezing with noticeable pressure. It wasn't a gesture of affection, he sensed, rather she was steering him to turn and exit with them. And as much as the prospect thrilled him—an after hours party at a notoriously hip club—he didn't feel he owned the skills such an improvisation required. Two movie star entrances? In one night? He didn't even know the layout of the place. Still, she'd asked him. And he could detect disappointment in their eyes when he said, "Some other time."

"All right, Curtis," Stephon said, removing his hand.

"Yeah." Teresa smiled as she walked away. Curtis could still feel the weight of her fingers on his shoulder. "See you Monday."

Monday. The word alone made Curtis cringe, though no one, he hoped, could see him. What was going to happen then, he wondered. He'd put so much attention on tonight. Had he forgotten about the rest of his life?

Where would he be without the music, the suit, the movie star entrance? His fingers moved busily as they hung by his sides, already calculating the number of days until he could at least wear the suit again.

Memory of his entrance to the Palmetto Room lingered for some time in the museum's offices. During the first few weeks afterward, rare was the day when someone, receptionist, gift-shop clerk, or preservationist, didn't ask Curtis about the party or inquire if he wanted to go to another one. But by the third week, few were making further inquiries, as he hadn't attended any of the gatherings. The dates were all too close to the first party, he surmised, and before his next appearance he really need time to plan. Still, another weekend passed and Curtis was alone in his apartment, unable to determine what he might do if another invitation were offered. The four hundred and fifty dollar outlay had devoured nearly all of his credit card balance, thus, the new outfit he imagined—a seersucker with pink stripes and white bucks this time—was one he could not purchase. Nor could he afford another session with Miriam and Ramon, at least until he'd gotten a paycheck and reduced his Master Card debt. But more than his limited funds, what frustrated him most was that all he could imagine was a variation on Miriam and Ramon's theme. Alone, he could not capitalize on whatever his Movie Star Entrance had given him in the eyes of his peers. He tried to compose a testimonial, hoping this might impel him toward a new line of thinking, but after one paragraph—"Before Movie Star Entrances, I used to be the kind of guy you noticed for a moment, but wouldn't remember"—he could go no further, convinced that without the suit and sound system, he still was that guy.

At the office, three weeks and four days after the

party, he tried a full day in the seersucker, which did resurrect some of the attention he'd received, yet most of it came from those whose time with him at the party was brief. Those like Teresa and Stephon, even Olga and Deena, as well, did not seem as impressed. When Teresa said, "Hey, there's *the* suit," Curtis could hear draining away in her voice any opportunity that she'd ask him to come along to Jamaica, Jamaica again.

There was but one solution. To go back to the experts, Miriam and Ramon. On a Friday, payday, Curtis found their card and dialed the number. Ramon answered and Curtis said, "Hey, Ramon." But before he could explain his predicament, Ramon whispered harshly, "I told you not to call this number. She answers it, too." Then he hung up.

A second call and a plea for Ramon to hang on gave Curtis the opportunity to explain, but all Ramon said was, "I'm not making any promises." As his ambivalence was far better than anything Curtis had summoned, at the end of the workday, Curtis was fighting traffic on I-10, headed again for the strip mall.

"We've always only done entrances," Ramon said. "We leave it up to the client to take it from there." Curtis nodded, keeping his eyes open, as if waiting to hear more than those same sentences Ramon had already said twice since Curtis's arrival. He and Ramon were seated at the cluttered desk at the rear of the shop, while Miriam prowled nearby, silent and intently smoking. Ramon opened a drawer, pulled out a bulky manila folder and dropped it on the desktop. "Over three hundred clients since we opened," he said. "No demand for money back. No complaints. And no one wanting to know what to do next."

"There's always a first," Curtis said, smiling and

shrugging. Throughout the drive over, his faith in Ramon and Miriam acted as much as an accelerant as his foot on the gas pedal. They'd brainstormed before and transformed him into the man who'd entered the Palmetto Room to such acclaim. Surely, they knew how to keep that man alive and help him take his next step forward? Curtis reached a damp, shaking hand toward Ramon's soft and manicured fingers. "Don't worry about the money," he said. "I expect to pay the full price." He swallowed. "More, if you want."

Ramon leaned back in the creaking desk chair. "Mr. Jenkins, you don't seem to understand. Miriam and I give you the entrée. That's it. You're the one who needs to find this 'next step,' as you put it."

Blinking, Curtis turned and looked to Miriam. The lights were as dim as his first time here, so he could only make out the barest outline of the angular woman. She'd yet to say a word and made no sound now save for hissing breaths of smoke. Sweating under his arms and at the small of his back—his AC was definitely running out of Freon—Curtis turned back to Ramon, clad in sandals and madras Bermudas that showed off his hairless calves. A pink Polo shirt with a white tennis sweater tied over his shoulders completed the outfit. The vision of him, as brown and fat as a Buddha, his black hair glistening with gel, along with the curious phone call they'd shared less than two hours ago, made Curtis recall his initial impression of Ramon's sexuality. He reached beneath his legs, raised his rear, and tugged forward the folding chair. "I'll do anything," he said, trying to deepen his voice and make it inviting. "I mean that." He blinked, wondering if Ramon could even see all this flirtation.

"We have six other clients right now. Six! And a fellow from Baytown—three hundred if he's a pound—who's costing us a fortune on fabric alone," Ramon said. He reached in the same open drawer and removed three plastic Solo cups and a half-filled bottle of tequila, Herradura. "I hate that you came all the way out here for nothing. And I need one of these." He grabbed the squarish bottle in both hands and poured.

"Salut," Ramon said, handing over a cup. "I wish there was something more we could do."

Curtis looked at the cup, lifted blue plastic rim to his dry lips and drank. The tequila splashed down the back of his throat smoothly, but it didn't quiet the thoughts in his head. Nor did it make him want another drink that might. All he could say was, "Nothing. No ideas? Not even a thought?"

Sighing, Ramon leaned forward in his seat. His rubber soled sandals slapped against the cement floor and he stood. "If we could, Mr. Jenkins, we would. But we've got to worry about Tubby from Baytown. I bet we don't even make a dime's profit from him." He gestured toward an alley between two rows of military costumes. Curtis set his cup next to the bottle and stood, but he was not ready to follow Ramon. He was searching the movie posters and props to spark his imagination, when Miriam stepped out from the shadows, inhaled on her cigarillo, and said through the smoke, "There is one thing."

As if someone had pulled a gun, Curtis wheeled around. "What?"

Miriam drew closer. She was wearing clogs and a long plaid skirt, like a preppie girl from Grinnell or Coe, as well as a monogrammed sweater with an upturned Polo collar around her reed-like neck. A strange outfit for any time of year in Houston, he thought, squinting to see that the monogram across her chest read, "S-E-X."

He swallowed. The inside of his nose tingled, and he reached inside his pocket for the right handkerchief. A few minutes ago, he was prepared to join Ramon in whatever act he desired, yet it felt far stranger to imagine Miriam as a potential partner. In his year in Houston, he'd been to bed with no one other than himself and worried he wouldn't be up to the level either one or both needed to get what each wanted. Miriam dropped the cigarillo to the floor, but didn't step on it. A thin ribbon of smoke curled upwards as she said, "Caan in *Godfather One*, Beatty and Dunaway in *Bonnie and Clyde*, Dafoe in *Platoon*."

"Huh," Curtis said, stepping back and wiping his nose with his handkerchief.

"Miriam," Ramon said, passing by Curtis and brushing against the clothes on the rack. The hangers clicked together, as Ramon said, "You aren't. Are you?"

"Pacino in *Scarface*," she said. "Washington in *Malcolm X*." She said more, named stars Curtis didn't recognize. Her tone achieved the kind of steady drone of a chant designed to summon dark and fell spirits. At last, she paused, then she and Ramon both said quietly, "The Movie Star Exit."

Now it was dawning on Curtis: in Miriam and Ramon's minds, the middle—what Curtis wanted—was tedious and dull. The perfect match to one of their entrances—it was theirs, after all—was an equally stunning exit. And in this case that would be accomplished by a violent and bloody death. "You don't mean," Curtis said, though he knew that's what they meant, and he couldn't quit envisioning all those aching angles of Bonnie and Clyde getting machine gunned. He knew when he saw the way their eyes found each other's. They looked at him only briefly. "You can't be serious," Curtis said, backing up a step and wiping at his face with the handkerchief, realizing too late it was the one he'd blown his nose with. "I mean."

But Ramon and Miriam weren't listening. Ramon was saying, "I can't believe you, you vixen."

"I've always wanted to do one."

"And you never told me?"

"It's a surprise, sweetie." Then she bent down and kissed him maternally on the nose. She raised her head, dragged her thumbnails slowly across another match. The flame lazily emerged, illuminating the lower half of her narrow face. She was smiling, and Curtis thought she also licked her lips. "What do you think, Mr. Jenkins? I guarantee your co-workers will be impressed."

She may have said more, but Curtis didn't hear, as he'd turned to run, stumbling at first and tangling his arms in the sleeves and legs of some of the costumes. Soon, though, he extricated himself. When he reached the door, he turned. They weren't following but Curtis still exited the shop as though he was in their reach.

At first he comforted himself with the fact that they did not know where he lived or worked. A look at the Greater Houston white pages revealed that there were twelve C. Jenkinses, making him grateful he'd chosen that more anonymous listing. The other Curtis Jenkinses numbered only two. If Miriam and Ramon were serious, they might tire after staking out the various men from Humble to Friendswood and League City. As well, Curtis had to ponder whether they were even serious at all. They'd always seemed odd—perhaps the strangest people he'd ever been acquainted with—yet not sociopaths, which they'd have to be to go through with such a plan. Perhaps they'd used it just to scare him out of the shop. Certainly he'd shown few signs of willingness to leave. But slowly, steadily, as no solution appeared in his thinking, and he saw nothing around him to steer him toward one belief or the other, thoughts of what might happen next began to consume him.

It didn't matter where he was or what he was doing. At work, home, driving to and from: always he moved as one who believes himself under ceaseless surveillance. Every step he took had behind it at least an hour of planning. He dressed so as not to stand out or garner attention. He used full service gas stations, always shopped at flagship grocery stores, and never went anywhere after dark. His parents left him long phone messages, which he didn't answer because he never answered the phone, lest a busy signal reveal to Miriam and Ramon that he was at home. He spoke of his distress to no one. Who'd believe him? And wouldn't his admission that he'd been to Miriam and Ramon remove any glimmering memories of that one night when everyone wanted to be next to him? The obvious plan, to leave and never return to Houston, frustrated him, because he held fiercely to the notion that whenever he knew he was no longer in any danger, he'd still have the chance to become the person he'd been at the party, that night.

His work didn't drop off, as if the burden of never knowing when that awful moment might come—Would it be firearms? A slow acting poison? Or would knives do the trick?—made the daily tedium of budgeting and accounting for the museum's dollars more preferable than it had been before. As well, inside the museum—the one place he knew they wouldn't try anything—he felt the most safe, the furthest from scrutiny. At times, he'd set dates. That if nothing had happened by October 15th, he would return to his previous routine, but every deadline passed with nothing like a return to his former life, and as the months passed, followed by the first year anniversary, then the second year anniversary of his entrance to the Palmetto Room, it was as if he could no longer remember what he'd done or who he'd been before that day.

So when he spotted Ramon and Miriam hiding behind the hedge surrounding the employee entrance to the museum, he did not turn and flee or call for help from the authorities. In fact, he laughed. The pair was so conspicuous, dressed in all black as they were. He suspected they'd left their shop believing they resembled some famous duo from a black and white classic, but they looked more like Boris and Natasha. Their surroundings—verdant shrubbery, live oaks and crepe myrtles—demanded camouflage, but Curtis believed they'd let fashion overshadow function, this time.

It was almost nine o'clock and Curtis was not the only employee walking on the sidewalk some fifty feet from the door. Betty Huynh was there, as were Olga and Felipe, and Stephon, in his security blazer, was holding open the door for Deena. Though he saw each one of them, Curtis was mostly focused on the realization that Miriam and Ramon must have been monitoring him for some time, lying in wait to see when he'd grown lax, and of course they wanted the greatest audience they could get for their feat. Wasn't there also some symmetry in this, when compared to his Movie Star Entrance? But why now? This day?

He slowed down. He was about twenty feet away now and saw Teresa Peters waving to him. He held up his hand and paused, allowed her to walk before him and enter the door. He wanted all his coworkers out of the firing line and for Miriam and Ramon to have as clean a shot as they liked. He hoped in the two years that they'd been practicing, because as easy as it was to get a gun in Texas, neither of them ever appeared the type who knew how to use one. As he took another step, the thought occurred to him that it still might be a joke—albeit an elaborate one: that they had no intention of killing him, just enjoying a laugh from the look on his face. Whatever possibility, though, he was prepared. All his fears had vanished. For now he knew: that whether their guns were as real as the heat of the morning or dusty props, whether they were accurate or not, whether he lived or died, he'd be the subject of discussion for years.

Who Among Us Knows the Route to Heaven?

A better world awaits me.

So I once believed.

But as of today—the afternoon's event still fresh and impelling me to write—mine is a name to be added just below Cain's on the long list of disgruntled brothers. For though my kinship with our first fugitive is recent, and I never once, from his birth to the present, wished my brother ill or was indifferent to his life, today I know that his was the offering accepted.

Once it seemed he was the only friend I had. Yes, there were our parents, but as the children of a black father and white mother—biracial, I believe, is the word—we were, at his birth in 1971, in suburban Central Ohio, a rarity. Odder than two-headed calves, stranger than Uri Geller, who could bend spoons with his mind. At that time, I was four years ahead of my brother in American life, and thought it my duty to be more than merely a *sibling*—a figure to query about trading cards, tadpoles and the fairer sex; I had to be a role model as well as a sentinel as vigilant as any sword-bearing angel. For I'd already determined that someone like me was always treading a narrow and treacherous path—not unlike the tightropes stretched out over Niagara Falls, with jagged rocks to one side, angry, churning water to the other. White children admired me when I broke the tape well ahead of them in the fifty-yard dash, or leapt over them for rebounds at the schoolyard courts. Yet when I brought to lunch fried chicken or napped in history, they chuckled quietly and nodded at each other in affirmation that their parents and the TV were right about black folk. Black children touched their hands to my wavy, undoubtedly, "good" hair, and envied my light eyes and skin, but if I professed an admiration, say, for the music of Supertramp, or did not return immediately the affection of a black girl my age, they aimed at me the barbs their parents had taught them: "Tom" and "Traitor."

My parents, bless them, were no more experienced or wiser about these matters than I. They told me to think of myself as an individual and nothing more. I could be anyone and anything I wanted. Heard then and now, this soothing litany did nothing but confuse me. And until my brother's birth, I was on my own to navigate that slim and wavering wire.

Dare I say my decision to aid my brother was correct? I told him all my woes as soon as he progressed from the contented coos of a babe yet to wander far from home to the hesitant words of a confused kindergartner. And, initially, he seemed a willing listener. His forays into the world brought him back with experiences similar—but not quite—to mine. Where I was wrong was in assuming that he'd be behind me on the wire. But because I'd survived those obstacles and blazed a path, if you will, his was a broader and simpler thoroughfare to travel. This cheered me, for I then believed our paths would keep us close together, and our reward was but a few paces ahead.

Had our lives remained static, I believe we would be in good stead today, still the best of friends and calling each other on the phone or visiting to compare and praise our respective blessings. But an incident occurred, one that may seem nondescript and unthreatening, but is, I assure you, the single cause for our—or is it my?—present condition. The incident I write of is our parents' unexpected leap into technology. In our home, television's presence had been virtually unnoticeable: my parents kept in their bedroom a twelve-inch black-and-white *Emerson* that hummed and glowed and spat out its corruption only when either mother or father deemed a program worthy of the entire family's attention. The four of us assembled on the bed, we watched events of import. In 1974, Mr. Nixon's resignation; the Cincinnati Reds' World Series victory in 1975. I admit I enjoyed these moments, the family huddled together as if for warmth, viewing those events the U.S. seemed to promise as evidence of a better place for its citizens. But even as a youth I knew the commercials were abrasive, the situation comedies mere spectacles of vice, the dramas void of any conflict that *mattered*. Never once did I see a face or family that looked like mine. But then, on the evening after President Reagan's re-election in 1984—a period we might recall as "Morning in America"—not only were we the new owners of a 24 inch color Magnavox, but too a VCR, along with the coaxial cables to enshrine us as the first family on our block with HBO.

From that moment, my stewardship was rocked. Early on, viewing increased in the new location—the family room. Our parents, with thirty-one channels at their disposal, claimed there were now ample opportunities for young boys to look upon events historical, educational, and affirmative. My brother was thirteen then—a perfect age, it seems to me now, to be seduced from the path. Soon the sound of the set became steady; daily I watched him kneel three feet away from the screen. Yet it was not simply his vigilance there that troubled me. His behavior became impossible to predict. He puffed and painted himself into every leading man, game show host, and compensated endorser he viewed. His voice changed— not through puberty's whims, as mine had, but in mimicry of those hawking detergent, after-shave and world views.

"It's a beautiful day," I told him one summer afternoon, the bizarre antics of Lucille Ball reflected in his eyes. "We should get out and enjoy it."

"Gilligan is on in a few minutes," he said, moving close enough to the screen to leave behind a greasy forehead print.

"Why do you get so close like that?"

His response came by way of the volume button: Ms Ball's whine soon eerily transformed into something like the wails of the damned.

He needed, I felt, a brother's advice. "They're not real," I said.

"Who?"

"Those TV people. They're robots. Mannequins. Not real like mother and father and me."

"Exactly," he said.

I could tolerate no more: I wedged myself between him and the screen, then thrust my knees rudely into his face. He pitched over backwards, then regarded me not with he rage I expected, but with a grin like that of the demons summoned by Doctor Faustus. "What are you going to do?" he said.

"Turn it off," I said. "Now."

*   *   *

It didn't stay off. And before it always sat my brother. For a time he sported a handlebar mustache. Later, in a pair of mother's heels, he read aloud from L. Ron Hubbard's *Dianetics*. Some days he appeared corpulent; others, Republican. In our bunkbeds at night he spoke with equal facility of bank-robberies and the Loch Ness Monster. Yet these guises, shapes and voices evaporated when our parents were home: to them he hadn't changed a jot. His grades were still high. Friends from school visited often. At thirteen, he claimed he wanted to go to Cornell, major in Hotel/Restaurant Management. Yet I knew this behavior to be illusory, and saw my guardianship as the last fortification against the flood. It had to be stepped up, sharpened. I buried the remote deep in the catbox, and shredded like cabbage for slaw his *TV Guides*, hoping if the instruments of what seemed like worship were no longer within reach, his return—the real him—would be imminent.

I left books from my and our parents' shelves in clear sight: biographies of Martin Luther King, Robert Kennedy and Kareem Abdul-Jabbar; novels by Baldwin—father's favorite writer—and the poetry of Nikki Giovanni, whose mother our mother once worked with. From the closet I retrieved the basketballs and baseball gloves, football cleats and ice skates. The board games. Ham radios. Jigsaw puzzles. Each I found where I left it.

Nothing could keep him from the set, bathing his ears in the balms of "Come on down!"; "Where's the Beef?"; and "No new taxes!" Thus when I turned eighteen and decided to begin my adulthood away from home, my guardianship—so long ignored and neglected—ceased. Who was I to think I could change him when he shined his jackboots, spoke in tongues, or masturbated fiercely? It was all I could do to walk out the door, while he took his eyes away from the transvestites on Phil Donahue, to reveal the still-beating heart of a dove rolling over the points of his sharpened canines.

My chief emotion when I thought of my brother had been regret. He was, undeniably, lost. When the scales fell from mother and father's eyes and they finally noticed this transformation, his would be a story of much sadness. Ten years I waited for some word of him; those same ten years I thought it best to never hear word of him: were that to occur, it meant for me visions of wreckage and ruination, stations I never once wished for him. As a result, I became more or less orphaned, without a sibling, wandering alone on the path I thought virtuous, only to find myself as far from a better world as I once thought my brother. In Houston, Texas I landed, whose skies are lit by distant fires (chemical plants, they say, but I know otherwise), where I am presently engaged in road repair for the county. I often wonder whether it was the falls or the rocks that I plunged toward, but to mull over that dilemma, tracing each step that was sure and each one that failed, is as torturous as the actual trek.

So it should not have surprised me this afternoon, when I, with a duffel bag of filthy work shirts and jeans, ventured to the Fairview Washateria, and saw on the other side of the Emerson anchored to the ceiling my very own brother. Thought most viewers registered his handsome looks, heard his resonant voice deliver an informed, even clever, report of a tornado's touchdown outside Channelview, I heard the message he had strictly for me. Peering through that crowd of citizens with dirty socks and quarters, he spotted me with eyes that were not his own, and told me, in a voice as borrowed as the suit he wore, that his election is secure, that he pities my lowly estate.

And at that moment, I knew he would live forever.

The Finest Writers in the World Today

To tell the truth, at first none of us believed there was money to be made from Tina Prescott's idea. Cause Celebs had been around for two-and-a-half years and was doing well enough to have five agents and about a hundred lookalikes because we understood our audience. They were people who wanted to bring pizzazz to the events in their lives, but on the cheap. For a nine-year-old's birthday, they couldn't afford the real article, so what about someone who resembled Brad Pitt? That was a different story. And though Cause Celebs wasn't the only agency in town, our lookalikes were dead ringers, as well as excellent vocalists and dancers. Or they wore great costumes and could lip synch.

Our performers broke down to two categories then. Dead celebrities was one: Charlie Chaplin, Marilyn Monroe, old and young Elvises and Sinatras—the perfect addition for your grandparents' anniversary! We also had contemporaries, which at the time meant Britney Spears, P-Diddy, Madonna, Bill and Hilary, both President Bushes. And they were all good, dead or contemporary. They made a nice flat fee, five hundred for three hours, out of which we took our thirty percent. No one was doing this full-time. They had daytime jobs and did their gigs at night or on the weekends. But everybody had a lot of work. Whether a corporation wanted to give some overworked execs a thrill—which is why that summer we had six Britneys and three Christina Aguileras—or a frat house wanted our Hail to the Chief Special, where Clinton and either of the Bushes pretended to wrestle. Every day of the week, we sent lookalikes out, at all hours. We delivered on time, with courtesy, and in the first year of operation secured our reputation for having the best damn celebrity lookalikes in Central Ohio.

Needless to say, when Tina made the suggestion, we didn't think our audience wanted writer lookalikes to grace their get-togethers. It just didn't seem something that would fly. Tina hadn't been one of we four founders. She'd come on first as a temp, showing lots of moxie and nutty ideas but doing no wrong, so we hired her permanently, promoted her to agent. At the time she was probably eager to show we had reason to keep her around. And new ideas never hurt. But she'd been an English major at OSU. You know the type. She was either scolding us about the movies we watched or the books we didn't read or hassling us about how Cause Celebs was a corruption of the actual French phrase. We knew that. All four of us founders had BBAs. Or she was saying our very service thrived on diseased obsessions with celebrity and that we needed to start doing something that enriched instead of poisoned the community. Generally, when she got off on topics like that, no one paid her much attention. Even the lookalikes. The CPA who played James Dean? He'd exit the office or duck behind a desk whenever Tina entered.

But it seemed harmless to let her set up auditions. After all, we agreed, as long as it didn't cost us anything, she could go ahead. Low costs had been our motto, which is why we only provided transportation and promotion for the lookalikes. Costumes, dance lessons, music, those were the lookalike's expenses. We did, though, make Tina promise she'd confine the auditions to two hours a day, to keep her attentions on other duties. And during those brief spells in the middle of the day it was funny to have these people coming in, funny because none of us knew who they were supposed to be. In rumpled clothes, unfashionable haircuts, they tramped in. Only Tina knew who they resembled, and even she made mistakes, guessing that the guy supposed to be Kurt Vonnegut was a young Mark Twain. (He didn't pass muster.) Everyone else in the office, the receptionists included, was expecting either the writer lookalike project wouldn't get off the ground or wind up a huge flop. Still, we were considering keeping a few. Having a Mark Twain or Shakespeare might class things up a bit or expand our clientele, all of us remembering a day in grammar school where we were visited by an actor playing Ben Franklin or Frederick Douglass.

Tina had other plans. After two weeks of daily auditions, she selected her writers, but when she told us the names, they were of people no one had heard of, let alone read anything by. Our ignorance made Tina furious. She stomped around the office saying, "She's only won a Pulitzer" or "Certainly, you've heard of the Nobel Prize!' She cheered up when she let us see her first ten lookalikes as if in a fashion show, each one walking through the office and back, holding a photo of the writer up to his or her face for us to compare. With the photos, we could see they were genuine lookalikes, evidence for that old saying that everyone has an identical twin. The best was a guy who resembled Bernard Malamud, who was ten years dead at the time. Tina, who seemed such a soft heart then, wouldn't turn the little guy down, especially when she discovered he was a retired jeweler named Murray Banks who'd lost his wife and was just coming out of his apartment again.

But as good as the lookalikes were, none of us expected a rash of requests for their services. We threw Tina a bone by adding to our radio ads and cable TV commercials a new voiceover claiming we now had lookalikes of some of the finest writers in the world today and at only half our typical price, but the phones, as they say, didn't start ringing. Months and months after the ads, we had our normal requests. We sent out six Britneys every night, the Hail to the Chief Special was getting a lot of action, too. For New Year's, we even expanded our classic celebrities with an act of high schoolers who did the Four Marx Brothers. But no writers got called. Tina showed no sign of panic, though. Every day she arrived at the office in her customary all black, her severe bangs and chalky makeup, an outfit that made us think she modeled herself after some obscure celebrity from the past we were too dim to have known. And she kept assuring everyone that with the ads a new audience would be discovered, as people who didn't have access to the real writers would turn to the writer lookalikes and soon after Cause Celebs would be finally close to doing some good for the world.

In a few more weeks, we started to get some requests. Not many, though you would think from Tina's reaction that they'd topped Britney and Christina. The one requested most was the Alice Walker lookalike, and she went to elementary schools and junior highs and a few writing clubs at the local colleges. Finally, it dawned on us that it was February, Black History Month, which also explained the increase in action for our Tina Turner, Bill Cosby and Snoop Dogg. So no one expected this trend to last or expand to the other writers. But by March, more and more of the writers were coming to the office with our percentage. It still wasn't a lot of money. We didn't think it time yet to bump up the appearance fee. No one was thinking about scrapping the project either. Though the writers could be a little irritating, hanging around and saying, "Are you sure you don't have a job for me?" John Irving always wanted to wrestle and William Burroughs was just plain creepy. But Bernard Malamud was the worst, hanging out in the reception area in a suit and tie—looking exactly like the writer, down to his mustache and glasses—then leaving with a heavy sigh when we shut down for the day.

Soon, in April, though, a real change of events occurred. A writer, a real one, was coming to town to give a speech at one of the colleges. (No lawsuit's been filed yet, but our lawyers tell us now it's best not to use her name.) It was pretty big news. The paper included a notice about the speech in the weekly cultural calendar and a blurb in the Sunday Arts page. We knew we had the writer's lookalike in our stable, but no one expected a call from OSU's new Dean of Humanities, who wanted, as a little joke, to have the lookalike show up at a reception after the writer's speech. Our lookalike, Myrna Boyd, was a friend of Tina's—another English major with no job—and a real piece of work. She'd never been sent out once in those first few months, yet she often sat around the office, demanding our receptionists run out to get her coffee, while she and Tina talked about how things were about to break for them. When she got this assignment, she tried to play it off as though it was no big deal, but the day of her appearance, she and Tina huddled in Tina's cubicle with a stack of the real writer's books and enough costume changes for the cast of *The Ten Commandments*. We all tried to tell her not to get too anxious. The Dean would pay for the full three hours, but he only wanted a little of Myrna's time for his joke to play out. Still, over coffee and cigarettes, Myrna and Tina prepared as if for a Broadway debut.

No one's absolutely sure if all that work was necessary. No doubt it helped that by the reception the writer herself hadn't made the best impression on her audience. News was she spoke so quietly that even with a microphone no one further back than three rows could hear her. And those who could hear didn't comprehend. Something about the corruption of the American Imagination was the subject, which sounded like a huge downer, to say the least. Worse still, at the reception, for which people had shelled out a hundred bucks to get stingy glassfuls of wine, steam table snacks and conversation with this writer, she was just as inaudible and uncommunicative. She'd say yes to a paragraph long question or stare over her glasses at people, then fire intimate questions about their sex lives and toilet habits. Things were bad at first for us, too, since Tina and Myrna got lost—and they were OSU alums—causing a late appearance for only the second time in Cause Celebs' history. (The first happened during a tornado warning, and our Sammy Davis Jr. still made it to the Jewish Retirement Home only ten minutes behind schedule.) So the Dean's practical joke had lost its timing. We'd learn later he was considering paying us only half the fee.

Until Myrna arrived. And if you're to believe Tina and the other guests, it was like Myrna was the real writer, her entrance was so grand. Myrna wore an evening gown and gloves, making the writer's man's oxford and faded denim skirt appear even more shabby. Soon after, most of the guests were talking to Myrna, not just about how amazing the resemblance was, but about the writer's latest books and her life story. Questions they'd already asked the real writer. Myrna reveled in all the attention, told anecdotes, got a little drunk and flirty, and even though she never came face to face with the writer, she charmed the Dean of Humanities so much he scheduled her to come next week to meet with his graduate seminar on the Contemporary Novel. No one found out what the writer had to say about the evening, as she sat alone for some time after Myrna's arrival, scribbling on napkins and eventually, around midnight, one of the waiters mentioned he'd seen her outside hailing a cab.

At Cause Celebs, we capitalized with newspaper ads featuring a testimony from the Dean, radio and TV spots concentrating on our writers. Before this promotion, though, requests were coming in. Our original audience wasn't changing their tastes in lookalikes. We never let go any of our old stable. Many still worked the same number of appearances during this heady time. What we had on our hands—as Tina had promised—was an entirely new audience that was growing. English departments from all over Ohio were calling, as were small bookstores and rural libraries, and, surprisingly, writers themselves. Either they wanted to multiply their appearances on book tours or they wanted to stay at home and write while a lookalike read before ten people at Book Warehouse. We got two messages from a Tom P., but no one in the office had heard of him. Tina was out with Myrna for a two-hour lunch—as they often were after their shared triumph— and much to Tina's chagrin, the memos with his number got misplaced by the time she returned.

But the majority of requests came from the publishers. It seemed there was a great need for author appearances—more than any of us, except Tina, had imagined—but at the same time a general disappointment from the audiences. One guy told Tina the disappointment had to do with the intimacy of books, how people manufactured a writer in their heads while reading, and that image could never be matched by the real person, who likely had long nose hairs or a whiny voice or wasn't able to look people in the eyes. So that's where our lookalikes came in: they could be whoever you wanted them to be.

Our lookalikes were more dependable, too. You got a guy who shows up everywhere stumbling drunk, you call in our guy: he's sober as a judge. A mumbler's work gets read by our straight-talker. The letch isn't around to pinch anyone's fanny. And the Prima Donna who won't read at Barnes & Noble because they uproot independent booksellers can stay home while our lookalike reads at WalMart! In the first few months after Myrna's appearance, more books were selling and readings were better attended than they'd ever been. We even made it possible for Knopf to showcase this Marquez fellow, who was a friend of Castro (we had a lookalike of him too, nice guy named Manny) and couldn't come to the U.S. Tina found the manager of a Mexican restaurant near Clintonville, dressed him up, and with a Latin American Lit Professor, wrote this guy some speeches and sent him out to thirty cities in thirty nights.

Everything was happening so fast, though, that with five of us concentrating on the writers, we still couldn't keep up. Our stable of writer lookalikes increased to keep up with demand, so there were auditions to sit through. We had to change our appearance structure and rate. No more three-hours a night, sometimes we were hiring people out for months at a time. We looked into the possibilities of opening offices in other cities. We hired new people to manage the celebrity lookalikes but still found more requests than we could handle. An article on Cause Celebs appeared in *Poets & Writers* about this time, claiming, "The bestseller list is no longer the benchmark of literary success. Now the measure is do you have a lookalike? And how many?" Dead writers were coming into vogue, which gave us an opportunity to send out Burroughs and Malamud. The Malamud lookalike was fantastic—a dead on mimic of the guy; the writer's book sales increased even more than when he'd won a Pulitzer. And every now and then, we four founders were pausing to look at one another with astonishment. We never talked about what was happening, though, as if we feared that might bring the magic to an end.

Some rival agencies tried to cash in on our success, but we had all the contacts, so there wasn't that much competition. The lookalikes themselves kicked up a little fuss after a while. Lead by Norman Mailer's lookalike—that fat little rabble rouser—they demanded we reduce our thirty percent take, which we did, settling on fifteen and overlooking that we still handled their transportation and already paid a generous per diem. More articles appeared, most in business journals praising us, some in literary magazines, where the knives were out. But even when those writers claimed our lookalikes were making writers obsolete and valuing celebrity over achievement, they weren't read by many people, and the issue stayed alive for the paying public.

Next came some heat from the real writers. Not all of them, of course. Some of our best customers were writers. But a lot complained they were getting cut out of the money. They earned more royalties from sales, but got nothing from the appearances in bookstores. They felt they deserved at least a percentage of what the lookalikes made, as the lookalikes profited on images that were rightly the property of the writers. Lawsuit threats were heavy at this point, but our lawyers kept us confident that no causes of action existed. The problem was not were we profiting on their celebrity, rather who created celebrity in the first place? Was it the celebrity or the audience? And who really could claim ownership of an image? A personality? Sure, they and their publishers owned the books, but, we would have argued, we were making the writers famous because of the lookalikes. We felt pretty secure around this time, smug because we'd triumphed over all the competition and complainers, but we weren't watching our real enemy at work: Tina.

Success had made her more intolerable than she'd been before. When she did come to the office, the time she spent there was brief, and she'd stopped communicating face to face. One day, she said nothing when she passed all four of us on her way in, trailed by a reporter from *People* and another from *Vogue*. Moments later, e-mails appeared on everyone's computer, reading: "Ms. Prescott apologizes for her brusqueness. She hopes soon to have time for all of you." Another time it was a fax, sent from her apartment, which was only three streets north. At the time, we would have said we were relieved to have her out of sight, but no one suspected she was in deep negotiations with William Morris and ICM, meanwhile telling all the lookalikes—we had two hundred and fifty now—that when she decided her next step, they'd all be coming wherever she went. "Ms. Prescott," read one of her e-mails, "wants nothing but the best for her discoveries."

This we ultimately learned from Malamud, who felt uncomfortable in leaving Cause Celebs, especially after we'd been so loyal to him from the start. Afterwards, we planned to confront Tina with the news, though by then it was likely too late. She was leaving. The question was when. Still, we needed to have our say, and when Tina showed up one Friday—almost a year later to the day she came to us with the writer lookalikes idea—we four stood in the office united, not letting her slip away. She was yammering on her cell phone headset, flanked by two burly lookalikes—John Irving and Eric Miles Williamson—cracking their knuckles like bodyguards. Tanned, hair bleached blonde, dressed in DKNY with pink and silver Nikes, Tina no longer looked like the temp who'd arrived with big ideas. We wondered if her black clothes, blunt bangs and white pallor had been a disguise all along. Now we had the real Tina. There were now serious doubts she was ever an English major. We asked if the news of her negotiations were true, and she sighed, gestured for Irving and Williamson to hang out in her office—no more cubicle for her—then said, "I knew this was coming."

"So what's the deal?" we asked. "You staying or going?"

"Going, of course," she said, as if there were no other options.

"What about the lookalikes?"

"Coming with me."

Now we had to try and shame her. "What about loyalty? Don't you remember how happy you were when you got hired permanently?"

"That was a long time ago," she said. "And you scoffed at every other idea I shared."

She had us there. Still, we tried flattery. "But we need you. You're the reason for our success."

"Too late. You should have said that long ago, when I worried you all thought I was a nut."

True, all true, so we fired our last weapon: guilt. "But what about the true meaning of the writer lookalikes? Wasn't it about bringing to the people the writers they needed to know? Wasn't it about improving the culture, not just profiting from its unhealthy fascinations?"

"Can't you do both?" Tina said, nimbly stepping

around us and heading toward her office for the last time. Before she reached the door, she stopped, looked over her shoulder. "Besides," she said. "You know if it had been your idea, each one of you would be doing exactly what I am."

True again. We four looked at one another, then watched Tina shut her door.

We're not broke. Operations are scaled back to what they were before and the fortunes of Cause Celebs are still strong. The need for celebrity lookalikes never ebbed, and we made sure to get paid while we did ride the writer lookalike trend that's become a tradition. Nowadays only the poets and most obscure or most famous writers— your Toni Morrisons and Philip Roths—do all their own readings. Everyone else has at least one lookalike, and if you hear yours isn't working, you'd better look for a teaching job. We flirted with trying to create a new stable of talent—Tina didn't own the idea—but like those agencies who tried to compete with us, we didn't know which writers to choose. Our Malumud, dear old Murray Banks, stayed with us longer than he should have, but now he's earning five figures a year and living on the West Coast, managed by Tina and Myrna, who's semi-retired as a lookalike. Supposedly she's working on a book of her own, a memoir, and only comes out for the big award presentations.

Still, there are times now when we pause from booking appearances for our Hail to the Chief Special— still a big winner—or giving W.C. Fields directions to a ninety year old's birthday party, we look at one another and it's easy to tell we're all recalling the thrills of our time at the top. It can be fun for a while, but soon it's back to work. You don't make any money recalling your last new idea. You've got to try and generate a new one. Right now, we can't claim any progress. But even though now and then you hear complaints, like the lookalikes don't really resemble the writers as they once did, and that the next step in publishing is to eliminate the writer altogether and just have legions of attractive folk with winning personalities to stand behind lecterns to read a computer program's words, even still, we like to think Cause Celebs will always be remembered. It's certainly not bragging to say we helped bring some needed changes to the world.

The Hotel Joseph Conrad

It is the most exclusive location I know. Its address is elusive, its guest list obscure. One assumes the interiors are palatial, the rooms filled with furnishings and *objets d'art* from the corners of the globe. The service must be efficient, if not embarrassingly obsequious, the meals prepared as for the royalty of fairy stories. I want to believe I am nearing it, whether the doors are trimmed in gold or as plain as the table on which I'm writing, though I may be as far away now as I was when my quest began. Still, I continue, hopeful one day to find myself within it, the Hotel Joseph Conrad.

Nearly five years ago, my agent contacted me with an offer that sounded so lucrative yet so simple, I first thought it a joke. Five thousand dollars, in advance, plus travel expenses, to write for a glossy magazine a thousand word article on the Hotel Joseph Conrad. Sally, my agent, handed me the contract and cashier's check, sent by the editors of *Excursions* to show they were, as stated in their letter, "most serious about the arrangements."

"Why me?" I asked Sally, a savvy New Yorker with

DKNY or Prada for each day of the week. "Why not Kennard or Fuller?"

"Read the letter, Maurice," Sally said, for once enunciating my name in the British manner my parents and I preferred.

The paper on which the letter was printed appeared like parchment and bore an elaborate letterhead, with a figure rather like Hermes toting a roller suitcase as its logo. (Why a wing-footed god needed wheeled luggage, I never asked, and now feel was a sign that should have worried me.) In rather formal but still very American English, the editors requested my services and praised my work, which consisted of a slim memoir (that sold to few besides friends and family) and six pieces on overseas travel. Presciently, the editors of *Excursions* answered my question of "Why me" in the penultimate paragraph: "Your recent experiences abroad—and your remarkable accounts of them—along with your youth as the son of an African diplomat and a Swedish mother, assures us you are *the* [their emphasis] writer for this task."

I stopped reading and turned to Sally. "Have you heard of it?" I said. "The Hotel Joseph Conrad?"

"I think A.B. Fields may have mentioned it once," Sally said. She blinked, tapped her blunt, red fingernails against the walnut top of her desk, then turned. Behind her stood a floor to ceiling shelf of books. Most were authored by her clients, though interspersed throughout was a volume or two by the acknowledged masters. Often, I hid a smile after seeing my last name on a spine between *Things Fall Apart* and *Winesburg, Ohio*.

"Fields," I said, impressed. Though deceased, A.B. Fields still commanded attention in the literary world, with three unfinished novellas that a pair of scholars and a book doctor labored to ready for publication. Having Fields and his estate as a client allowed Sally to keep non-remunerative writers such as myself in her stable, a fact for which I was more than grateful. For now, though, I watched Sally tap a finger along her books and thought about this hotel I'd never heard of. I then gazed at the magazine. The cover featured a photograph of two tiny figures at the foot of a mammoth waterfall, with the title, "Hidden Amazon." I leafed through, recognizing none of the authors who penned essays on undisturbed natural paradises and furtive regions of the man-made world. So I closed *Excursions*, picked the check up by its top left corner.

"Here," Sally said, handing me a hardback with soft corners and a loose spine. I reached for it with my other hand, saw it was *The Nigger of the Narcissus*, a book I'd yet to read. "Sorry," Sally said. "It was the only Conrad I had."

I smiled. "I've been called worse."

"Still haven't read the whole letter, have you?" Sally said, returning to her desk chair. Her smile was smug. She knew something I didn't. After setting the book and the check on her desk, I resumed reading the letter. Then I saw the information no writer could reject. The agreement was to last five years, with travel reimbursed and money arriving—lessened by a thousand dollars each year—until delivery of the article. "I don't need the money," I said, a half-truth at best. Then I held up the check to find its watermark.

"Still," Sally said. "Don't you want to at least see this place?"

I folded the check, fitted it into the breast pocket of my blue blazer. "Answer your question?" I said.

Sally stood, squeezed my arm. I said, "Where's the flight information?"

She let me go. "There isn't any."

"Must be waiting until the contract arrives."

"You're probably right," she said and touched the side of her face.

I uncapped my pen, signed and initialed three places

on the contract. Again, Sally handed me the Conrad book, told me it was mine to keep, then called in an assistant. To me, she said nothing more, and I folded my copy of the contract and the letter into the book, then departed, certain the tickets—whether for a jet, locomotive or dhow—would soon arrive.

Of course, none came. The check cleared, however. Acknowledgment of the contract's receipt was faxed to Sally, along with a typed note encouraging me to get started in autumn, when the Hotel Joseph Conrad was "a spectacle that demands to be seen." But no information arrived to indicate which direction I should take to get there. Hindsight tells me I should have inquired into *Excursions* more fully—I never saw another issue—or interrogated Sally and the staff. Even now I'm not sure if she had motives other than at last making some regular money off me. I was no investigator, though. I was a writer, who mostly wrote about myself and what I'd done. So I focused my energies on finding anything I could about the Hotel Joseph Conrad. No web search returned any information. None of my friends—writers, artists, diplomats' children—had heard of it, and many had traveled up one side of the globe and down the other. Of one thing I remained certain: The Hotel Joseph Conrad wasn't in the United States, my home of the past ten years. I suspected this because of the syntax, knowing few places between Bakersfield and Boston that didn't have "hotel" in the posterior position. Still, that left a lot of territory. Though my travel expenses would be reimbursed, I didn't want to start jetting about and wasting time—there were other things I'd been working on: a manuscript that hadn't decided if it was memoir or fiction, an essay about being the citizen of many nations but not one. So I turned to what I felt was the proper course: Joseph Conrad.

I was, I should say, no Conrad aficionado, the prime reason I'd wondered why I'd been selected by *Excursions.* In school, I'd read *Heart of Darkness*, *The Secret Sharer*, *Lord Jim* and admitted to myself, tutors and peers, that the man's prose style was remarkable for its power and clarity as well as the fact English was his third language. But as the son of an African—even a diplomat who himself was the son of a doctor and a professor—I couldn't eliminate from my reading of Conrad a distaste for his depiction of people of color. Yes, I could consider the time in which he wrote and compare him favorably to his contemporaries, and while I was certainly not in Mr. Achebe's camp, willing to consign Conrad's work to the heap, I cringed every time an African appeared in his pages. And at thirty-five—my age when this saga began—I wasn't in a rush to resume that experience, even with Sally's copy of *The Nigger of the Narcissus* on my desk. Instead, I looked to the biographies, buying Professor Karl's doorstop and three slimmer ones, to give myself a suitable list of places to confine my search. My logic held that the Hotel Joseph Conrad must be tucked away on an isolated street in one of the cities he'd lived or visited. And it had to be a place that would see fit to honor the man, which made it easy to overlook Africa, South America and Asia. But I was fortunate, I thought then, as I didn't have to complete this task straight away. I had ample time and owed *Excursions* only a thousand words. Still, my mind was set on finding the hotel. Even as a child, I'd been committed to completing tasks, earning a reputation among my schoolmates for single-mindedness. My present girlfriend feared the project might distract me from what she called my "real work," but once I had my list in place, I didn't want to lie about. I started traveling, first to the Ukraine, then Poland and Southern France, all new places for me. Australia was next, followed by travels in Jamaica—where I was nearly run over by a taxi—then to the UK, where I visited the Conrad Society and talked to many fine and interesting scholars, but they, as did my parents, friends, and every single other human I'd asked during the past seven months, had no idea where one might find the Hotel Joseph Conrad.

Around this time, on long flights and during dull evenings in hotel rooms, I began reading Conrad's fiction, starting with the work I'd read before, then moving on to some I'd neglected: *Nostromo*, *Under Western Eyes*, *The Secret Agent*. Though I wasn't reading for appreciation—I was looking for names of cities and towns, *clues*—I'd every now and then be so moved by a description or insight into the psyche of a character that I'd uncap my pen and ink a thin line beneath the sentences. My girlfriend reminded me of the current critical approach to Conrad's work: good prose, execrable politics. I kept reading, finding many hints but nothing that showed me the way. One thought I had was that with Conrad's nomadic existence and his service as a seaman, the appropriate venue for a hotel named in his honor was a ship of some sort, with enormous suites, endless buffets and a passenger billet so short that the staff outnumbered the guests twenty to one. Searching through all the registers of ships and ports of every sea showed me nothing of the kind. Had I another project to escape into, I might have ended my research, but the narrator of my memoir/novel stopped talking, and my unfinished essay seemed unbearably thin. I carried on.

Then, all of a sudden, I drew nearer. In Paris, where my girlfriend and I were on holiday. The trip wasn't my idea. I'd been to Paris before, several times as a matter of fact. But my girlfriend demanded we go. I needed, in her words, to get my mind off of Conrad. And for the most part I did. Paris was as it had always been: one leisurely opportunity followed by another. A morning in the café, then splendid hours in the Louvre or D'orsay. Miraculous suppers with marvelous wines in dark bistros recommended by friends. One bright spring afternoon, though, nearly eighteen months after my visit to Sally's office, we strolled along the Ile de la Cite, finding ourselves near the Quai D'anjou. My girlfriend was reading aloud from a guidebook when she pointed to a rather plain building and said it had formerly been the offices of *transatlantic review.* Had I not been reading so much about and by Conrad, I might have been interested enough to stop or take a photograph, but the coincidence struck me with some heat. You know the foolish notions that come to one sometimes. Conrad himself wrote that, in *Heart of Darkness.* Yet on one of the few occasions I wasn't trying to locate the hotel, we passed the former offices of a magazine that published Conrad's work. As soon as I had the chance, I hurried us two back to our hotel in the eleventh arondissment, then claimed there was something I wanted to see for myself. "Joseph Conrad," my girlfriend said, uttering the name like that of a woman with whom I'd had an affair.

I said nothing but left nonetheless, returning to that majestic island in the Seine to harass passersby with my schoolboy French. Each time I asked, "Ou est l'hotel de Joseph Conrad?" I earned looks of concern or contempt, and my heart sank in my chest. What did this behavior reveal about me, I wondered. Shouldn't I be back in a real hotel, making love to my tall and willowy girlfriend? In Paris? In Spring? Then a young North African in a red jacket approached me. I hadn't spoken to him, yet he was smiling and saying, "Hotel Joseph Conrad? *Allons! Vite, vite.*"

My heels hammered the cobblestones as I followed him. Nimble as could be, he faced me while running backwards, pointing at his close-cropped head and mine, smoothing his hand over the exposed flesh of his forearms, calling attention to our similarities, I believe. When I asked how he knew of the hotel, as I could translate, he claimed to have worked there at several banquets—*tres elegant*, he vowed—and had been sworn to secrecy as to its location and guests. A falling out, however, had gotten him sacked and three weeks hence he'd received not a sou. As I lurched past Parisians and tourists, I marveled at how my stumbling upon this discovery seemed so—what else could it be—Conradesque. Briefly, I lost track of my young guide and raced forward, nearly upsetting a pair of Japanese girls in plaid skirts. Ahead, I saw the young man's red jacket, Puma spelled out in white on the back. Breathing hoarsely, I pulled up beside him and clapped my hand on his shoulder. I didn't much like the look on his face, foreshadowing, if not duplicating, the disappointment that spread over my own. "*Ici*," he said, pointing to a door that looked like the ones on each side of it. "*Ici*." He pushed it open and a hallway led to an open area that did, I'll admit, display the marks of a recent and thorough cleaning. Yet no concierges manned desks in a dazzling lobby, no busts of Conrad stood nearby, no portraits hung from the wall. "It was here," the boy said in schoolboy English, far better than my schoolboy French. I shook his hand and nodded, inhaling dust and coughing. Sore footed, lungs aflame, I limped back to the Metro. To make matters worse, when I returned to my hotel—its existence as undeniable as the Eifel Tower—my girlfriend had left me a note. I still have it, and read, from time to time, her message: "You're having your fun. I'm out having mine."

Much could explain the incident in Paris. A problem in translation, for instance, or a boy's elaborate practical joke. When I returned to Manhattan, however, and moved from my girlfriend's apartment to an illegal sublet in Hell's

Kitchen, I did not yet consider there was someone or a group who wanted me to gad about the globe in search of some nonexistent hotel. I considered the folly that I had neared the hotel—it was where the North African boy said—but through some extraordinary feat, the hotel staff had picked up and moved everything from candlesticks to king-sized beds to another location. Whom was I kidding? Time passed. I did not renew my search, reminding myself on the second anniversary of signing the contract that I still had ample time. A check arrived from Sally's office and cleared easily. I did my best to spend the money.

Meanwhile, no other writing projects inspired me. The primary subject of my work had always been my life, and not only had I failed to interest a reading public, I no longer interested myself. Friends called. My parents, as well. All wanted to know what I was doing, and I obliquely said, "Working," though some days I barely found energy enough to shower. In the fall, I got going again, traveling to South America and finding nothing but receiving in envelopes with no return addresses the amount of money to the penny that I'd used to get myself up and down the coast of Brazil and the interiors of Argentina. Back home, I reviewed my single copy of *Excursions*, then hurried to the Brooklyn address where their offices were purportedly located. The present tenants—a XXX DVD warehouse— thought there had been a magazine published here before but had no new address to direct me. Of course, I found no copies in the stores or libraries of New York—each and every borough—and started wondering what Sally knew when I commenced this quest.

My one solace, during this time, was the work of Joseph Conrad. Formerly, I'd believed the joy of literature was the spaces in books where I could find myself, the characters whose pasts summoned up my own, the events and locales like those of my own experience. While reading Conrad, though, *I* didn't seem to matter at all. *I* ceased to exist in his jungles and ships and elaborate adventure. I was mere witness to it all. After all the years of looking to writers of color for kinship, to ignore them for Joseph Conrad felt almost like betrayal. Yet in their work, I was utterly aware of my self, never got caught so deeply in the labyrinth that all I wanted was to learn what, just what, could possibly happen next. Some nights, I dreamed of us all at a banquet table, in fancy dress: Soyinka, Mishima, Rushdie, Allende, and Morrison, approached by a dusty, bearded figure from the turn of the twentieth century. All the writers of color then looked at me, their disdain as visible as it had been on my girlfriend's face in Paris. "Who invited him?" they said. And in the dream I could supply no response. In my waking life nothing dissuaded me from reading Conrad. In fact, my reading expanded, as I haunted libraries and used bookstores, searching for lesser known stories and later novels. I found myself slowing, reading a page in the time I'd normally read a chapter, delaying the inevitable running out of Conrad's work. Oh yes, I told myself, I could always return to prior books, but I knew then that while re-reading I would not find the discoveries I'd made the first time through. And now it seems so clear what I wanted then, above all else, was discoveries.

Nonetheless, nearly three-and-a-half years after my introduction to the Hotel Joseph Conrad had passed when Sally wangled for me a review article on the publication of A.B. Fields's posthumous trilogy of novellas. The project had taken so long to complete, I learned, because the scholars and the book doctor could come to little agreement over the editing. Each accused the other of diminishing the value of the work, the book doctor bemoaning that the scholars made the exciting books tedious, while the scholars charged the book doctor made the complex novellas into mere pageturners. At first, I wanted to say no—I didn't want to interrupt my reading of Conrad's last novel, *The Rover*—but Sally insisted, and I'd always enjoyed Fields's work. His early novels, in their intensity and focus on the nature of man, had earned comparisons to Conrad, and soon I discovered the editors had done a fine job with the novellas. With ten thousand words, however, I was expected to provide more than simple evaluation but an overview of the man's career and how these novellas fit into his oeuvre. To this end, I had access, thanks to Sally—about whom my suspicions quieted—to the man's journals and correspondence. A bachelor, Fields had no heirs to claim these materials. And just as I'd lost myself in reading Conrad, I swiftly lost myself in Fields's private reflections and confessions. Still, I maintained productive days: reading Fields's novellas in the morning, writing in the afternoons, then sitting down with Xeroxes of his journals and correspondence at night. On such an evening, I came across a reference that halted all progress on the review article. I stole the Xeroxed sheet from his 1967 journal but don't need it in front of me to accurately quote the passage: "December 3. Heard today some startling news. Alderson has been refused by the HJC. What a shame. The poor dope did all that work and never knew how close he was."

My head shot around as if I sensed I was being watched. But I was alone in my apartment, where the paint peeled, the taps dripped and the radiator groaned. For the first time, I entertained the fear I was the butt of an elaborate and expensive prank. Assembled against me were a host of people, including Sally and my ex-girlfriend, even the North African boy in Paris, all employed to keep me chasing the phantom of a ghost instead of writing. But what had I done to earn such attention? I wasn't famous or powerful enough to warrant such machinations. And to imagine my name had been randomly selected—out of the phone directory, if you will—who would go to such lengths to frustrate and encourage me through these

endless tasks? Now, though, with Fields's mention of the
Hotel Joseph Conrad (what else could the initials stand
for? Hicksville Junior College? Hallowed Jesus Christ?),
things made sense. The Hotel did exist. And for whatever
reason, I'd been selected to try and gain access to it. With
that realization warming my blood, though, another chilled
me: Alderson, whom Fields wrote of, had not gotten in.
Who was he? I resumed reading the journals but found
no further mention of him or the Hotel Joseph Conrad.

As I sat back in my hard chair, a hazy pattern
of the last few years emerged: Every point at which I
thought I was close, the object of pursuit stepped out
of sight. I'd been living a version of Zeno's Paradox and
would continue to near but never reach the Hotel Joseph
Conrad, whether it was a ship at sea, a portable hotel or,
as it seemed that evening (and early morning, as I did not
sleep), a small group of writers who effectively hazed
other writers to see if they had the stuff to allow them
membership among the elect.

As if a taunt, as if I were under constant surveillance,
the next afternoon my annual diminishing check arrived,
along with Sally's note reminding me I was now entering
my last year of the agreement, and if I didn't have the
thousand words turned in by this date next year, there
would be no more checks or travel reimbursement. I knew
not what to do, nor to whom to turn. Fields was dead,
I distrusted Sally. And Alderson: where was he? I feared
any step would put me in a spot like the one Alderson
had tripped upon, and the last years of my life would
always appear to me—and those who were watching—as a
colossal cock-up. Of course, I put aside the article. It only
lacked a conclusion, but I could not write another word
about Fields now. That afternoon, I managed to exit the
apartment and walk to my bank. The sidewalks appeared
occupied by pedestrians who looked away suddenly or
ducked into cabs that sped off. I reminded myself of

the little sleep I'd had, went into my bank to deposit the check, and earned the smile of a teller—an attractive Puerto Rican woman I'd never seen before—who asked me shyly what I did for a living. "What I do?" I found myself saying. She was flirting, perhaps, and it had been some years since another had showed me such affection. Yet I no longer felt like a writer, had nothing to produce that might establish my active credentials, so I looked at her, coughed, and said, "Seaman." I turned round. I wondered if the teller was now reporting to her contact my failure or success. I wondered if I'd ever be able to stop wondering about such things.

Two weeks now remain before the end of my fifth year. In the time since I received the final check, I have been to London three times, along with Opole and Krakow in Poland, Kiev and Berdichev in the Ukraine. Ask me about the tiniest of streets in any of those cities: I've walked them. Twice. I've scoured every dock from Manhattan to Marseille, have interviewed three former lovers of Fields—even kissed one of those septuagenarian crones—and pored through the archives of other writers for mention of the Hotel Joseph Conrad but have found none. About Alderson, it's as if such a writer never existed, the only evidence being a Midwestern college literary magazine with three poems about lacrosse by a Terry Alders, published in 1949. These failures heaped behind me, I should be depressed yet presently find myself stifling elation, writing less and less legibly as I struggle to an end of this account. When I began, I hoped that by setting forth these exploits on paper I would have a clearer sense of all that happened since that afternoon at Sally's office. (She's since moved, though before she did, I broke in to see if I could find anything incriminating. Another fruitless go.) I could no longer just talk about this saga to myself or friends or family—the latter for fear the membership committee of the Hotel Joseph Conrad might disapprove. But as I just re-read the opening pages here to find again my place after a few hours of exhausting, dream-riddled sleep, I have—I believe—lucked upon my solution.

The contract! I hadn't read it in years, just kept it tucked in *The Nigger of the Narcissus*, hidden, as it was, beneath notebooks, receipts, maps and itineraries. And as I hoped, the contract does not speak of *finding* the Hotel Joseph Conrad. I was asked only to deliver a thousand word article *about* it. "My task which I am trying to achieve is, by the power of the written word, to make you hear, to make you feel—it is, before all, to make you *see*." In the Preface to *The Nigger of the Narcissus*—the very book Sally gave me—Conrad wrote the former. And now I must make you—whoever "you" might be—see my Hotel Joseph Conrad. I can place it anywhere I like, make it as plain or as ornamental as I care, build it at sixteen stories or in the shape of a octopus, put bunk beds in each room and hot tubs on every other floor, hand out complementary silk pajamas and monocles, employ power trios or klezmer bands to play on the rooftop, hire peg-legged concierges and blind and mute bartenders who pour the coldest gin martinis known to man. Of course, even now, with sweaty, shaking hands, I can't be completely sure I'm right. I wonder if any others, this moment, are slaving after this same goal. Or am I the only one? If I fail might there be a place for me in the Hotel Ford Madox Ford? Whatever the case, I must bring this account to a close. I need every second of the time remaining and must write the finest thousand words I have ever composed. For this much I know: I must construct the Hotel Joseph Conrad to suit each and every one of my needs, for I will be in it to stay.

The Most Famous Man in These United States

I was the only adult in America who hadn't appeared on television, but a number of people were doing their best to change that.

First was my girlfriend, Rochelle, whom you'll no doubt recall from "But Would You Do it For Money?" She made the final round and would have won fifty grand had she summoned the will to re-ingest the pitcher full of partly digested french fries and warm draft beer she'd vomited just moments before. Yet her crucial failure of nerve in the spotlight had not dissuaded her of the medium's power. After weeks of hints and suggestions, one night while we were seated in our common places— Rochelle on the couch, me on the floor, my back to the TV—she said, "It'll get you noticed. Maybe that's what you need to help you with your music."

"You think?" I said. I still fancied notions of recording contracts, envisioned my name spelled out on marquees, but I'd been kicked out of every band I'd played in and had a hard time finding local clubowners who'd let me play a set before customers. The bulk of the wages, earnings and salary I'd entered on my 1040

E-Z came from teaching hollow eyed suburbanites how to thrash power chords like their idols from the music channels. Still, I was skeptical a TV appearance could help me. I said, "Isn't the old-fashioned way of practice, practice, practice more meet? Evidence of merit rather than crass fortune?"

I didn't believe this. Any short-cut to success offered was one I'd gladly take. What I presently wanted was to see Rochelle's eyebrows knit, which they always did when she didn't quite know the meaning of a word. I tried to determine which term, meet or merit, caused that lovely meeting of her sparse brows (a little browner now, as she was in between foils), but she shut her eyes, shook her head. She took my hand, pressed it against her chest. "Think what it's done for me," she said.

I did think about it—in between glances at her augmented breasts—then raised my eyes to examine her earnest face. She nodded preliminarily, as if to coax from me positive responses. Her brown eyes, blue behind contacts, grew round with pleading. She too was biracial, but with her creamy brown skin, and a hairstyle that looks windblown without nature's assistance, she belonged on TV. Far more than I, a skinny mulatto with a jaundiced complexion and teeth stained from the well water I drank as a child. However, her looks didn't distract me from my conclusion: her TV appearance hadn't done much. She returned from California with a year's supply of an herbal supplement subsequently banned by the FDA and a few anecdotes of sighting celebrities—"*Other* celebrities," she was fond of saying—on the other side of Rodeo Drive. And since, though it was common for her to sign autographs whenever we were out, she hadn't received a part in any of the independent films or regional plays she auditioned for. She'd even lost out an opportunity to model spring wear for a Dillard's commercial.

Unsure of what to say, I stammered until Rochelle

caught my chin in her hand, looked me in the eye, and said, "It brought us together." Then she kissed me. With her tongue swirling rapidly over my molars, I couldn't tell her I'd never seen an episode of "But Would You Do it For Money?" until after we met outside Juanita's. Before that moment, the only TV I viewed at all was the one bolted to the ceiling in the Heights' Laundromat. I decided to lose myself in the kiss, but allowed my hands to stray toward her shoulders, which caused her to pull back, her hands rising protectively to her head as she said, "My hair!"

Next was my mother. She called me to meet her for lunch at Sekisui—whose sushi was celebrated in Little Rock but quite counter to the deep-fried and gravy-covered cuisine my mother had served my older brother and I daily. I hadn't seen her in a couple of months, and her physical appearance surprised me. She was tauter around the neck and her eyes no longer looked so tired. I suspected cosmetic surgery, but my mother was busy making known that I needed to show Americans I was a capable individual, a valuable contributor to society, and my multi-racial family had been a help, not a hindrance. "I'm seeing too many freaks on TV lately," she said, suddenly expert with chopsticks and nimbly dunking smoked eel and raw tuna into shallow bowls of soy sauce. "Kids complaining about their parents, wishing they weren't born, that sort of thing. You need to show they're not the norm. You are."

I didn't tell her to quit watching TV, as I knew she needed the set on at all hours, even if she was in another room and could only hear its ghostly voices. I didn't mention my brother or his incarceration. Besides, rice was crumbling into my soy sauce and the chopsticks kept falling from my slippery fingers. I shifted my attention to the soybeans, popped one of the salty devils in my mouth, which caused my mother to say, "Shell it first, dear." She pointed to the pile of empty green skins neatly formed on her rectangular plate. "You'll show the world," she continued. "And help out all those biracial children who worry they're so alone and so odd. You should hear some of the stories I saw the other night on the news."

She had good intentions, my mother. But she and my father had had good intentions when they appeared on "Still Faithful After all these Years"—whose end punctuation, I know from Rochelle, transforms from ellipses to a question mark at the opening of the hour-long show. Because I never watched during that premiere season, I didn't witness the episode that captured the end of my parents' twenty-nine year marriage. I suppose it's entertaining to bring unwitting married couples together on a cruise ship under the ruse their unions are being rewarded, then, at the first port of call, introduce a corps of scheming single women—skanks, Rochelle called the women after she auditioned (and didn't get the part). And in fairness, next season's edition, according to Rochelle, promises hot guys as the bait. However, I didn't watch last year's reruns and see my father, the first husband to fall, succumbing to the wiles of the woman—a year and four months younger than I—he now lives with in Scottsdale, Arizona.

Nor would I remind my mother of this as she finished her sushi and started eating mine. My thoughts drifted to pulled pork sandwiches with slaw, while she said, "I think you'd make an excellent role model. Honest. Well-spoken. Respectful."

"Yes, ma'am," I said dutifully.

"Handsome, too," she said.

Though conscious of her flattery—my brother was the good-looking one—I turned to her my good side. "You'll do it then?" she said, summoning a single tear. "For me?"

I feigned a sneeze, another, then another and kept up the violent snap of my neck until my mother asked after my health. So much for honesty and respectfulness. By the time she'd become sure I wasn't experiencing some allergic reaction to the sushi, her request had become foggy, and I made sure she forgot by asking about her latest suitors. They numbered two, one an attorney, the other a golf pro—both famed locally for their obnoxious commercials—and she was happy to discuss the virtues of both while I pretended to listen.

My older brother was next. I had for him some cigarettes and old L. Ron Hubbard paperbacks he'd been asking for, and was headed to the reformatory anyway. But when he came to the other side of the plexiglass in the visitor's area, I felt uneasy at his carrying a phone-directory sized stack of papers. He looked well, as he always did, far better looking than I, with better posture, cleaner nails. For a moment, I envied him, then reminded myself who had to return to his cell in twenty minutes. I wonder what might have been his fate had he not become such a notorious crystal meth dealer that he landed on the local and national versions of "Crimestoppers, Inc." But even then, especially during his videotaped capture on his third and final appearance, he looked well-groomed and alluring, a fact borne out by the letters he showed me from his many female admirers.

Now, though, he set down the stack of paper on the ledge behind the plexiglass, greeted me, and said, "You still pretending to be a minimalist?"

His vocabulary—never his strong suit—had improved, but I imagined a dictionary and a thesaurus on his cot, both turned to the M's. "How so?" I asked.

"You still don't own a TV?"

"My girlfriend," I said. "She owns one."

"Rochelle," my brother said, stroking his chin as if to remind me how much more square and firm his was. "The one who flashed the Methodist convention and shaved the fat guy's ass but turned up her nose at the second time around with those fries?"

I mulled over some choice terms to describe him: fuck-up, dope dealer, convict. "The one and the same," I said.

"Well, she's not why I wanted to talk. You heard about 'Sibling Rivalry?'"

"Pardon?" I said, leaning forward. A guard walked near, reminded me that we had only fifteen minutes. As he returned to his post, I recalled his face—moreover, his enormous biceps—from a law enforcement arm-wrestling special Rochelle could not look away from, while I practiced scales.

My brother coughed, gained my attention. He donned a pair of glasses I'd never seen him wearing. He ran a palm over his graying hair. He began to read, haltingly: "Ever since the days of Cain and Abel, siblings have clashed against one another, over reasons as great as life or death or as petty as who gets the top bunk. Now, an opportunity exists for dueling siblings to fight it out, but within the ring, under the watchful eyes of skilled trainers and expert referees, who will ensure the safety of both participants. Got a beef with your brother? A spat with your sis? Well, let's get it on, then, on 'Sibling Rivalry.'"

"What is that?" I said.

"I knew you hadn't seen it." My brother sighed, shook his head at my ignorance. "It's 'Sibling Rivalry,' like I said. This show that lets brothers fight, for three rounds, under Nevada rules. Dr. Gillis, the shrink here, he says it sounds very therapeutic."

I really was stunned. So much so, that was all I could say: "I'm really stunned."

"Come on," my brother said. "It'll be just what we

need. I've had a lot of time to reflect in here and I think you and I have a lot of issues we need to confront."

Therapeutic? Issues? Confront? My brother didn't talk this way. Before his arrest his principal terms and phrases were "ounce" and "costs" and "It'll fuck you up." "What issues?" I said.

"Isn't it obvious, for one?" he said, motioning to my face, then dragging his fingers across his face and forearms, calling attention to the color of our skin, though his always appeared a warm caramel, especially in comparison to my sickly yellow.

"What else though?"

"I resent you. Your life on the outside. And I'm starting to wonder if mom and dad liked you best."

I summoned the memory of Xmases where he played with GI Joes, toy guns and football equipment, while I stared at clothes with growing room and books too young for me. The one gift I always wanted—a guitar—was never there. I had to save money from a fast-food job to buy one. "That's not even true," I said. "Mom and Dad doted on you."

My brother slumped in his seat, snatched off his reading glasses, then leaned forward. "Just say you'll do it. You don't know what it's like." His eyes looked red and genuinely weepy—unlike my mother's at lunch. (I suspected she had a tack in her shoe.)

"To be inside?" I said, wondering for a moment just how bad it might be. Never before had he complained, and during my visits the facilities resembled as much a dormitory at an alternative university as a house of reform.

He tossed his glasses on the ledge, shook his head. "No, to be on TV and not be able to get back. That high's stronger than any shit I ever sold." He grabbed the stack of papers, pulled out some documents. "Anyway, it's not just me. The warden would love to have the show here. My agent's worked it out so they'll tape live from the ring in the rec area. Isn't that awesome? All we need is your ok."

"Your agent?"

"Davenport. My lawyer. He's worked out deals for all his clients now."

As if projected onto the plexiglass, the image of the two of us in shorts, mouthpieces and oversized gloves shimmered before me. I shut my eyes. I wish I could claim nobility of mind, base my unwillingness to fight on my revulsion at the idea of two men of color— brothers!—about to fight for the entertainment of others. But in truth I knew after his time in the penitentiary, my brother would clobber me. I wouldn't even get in the one punch I'd wanted to throw for some time. So I stood, walked toward the exit without waving, and carried the shopping bag of paperbacks and cartons of cigarettes. "Wait," my brother said. "We don't even have to actually hit each other. A few weeks of practice and we can put on a good show where nobody gets hurt."

The guard with the massive biceps stood before me, blinking. "This is for him," I said, my back to my brother. The guard stayed with me until I reached the exit. While I waited to be buzzed out, he said, "He's right, you know. The warden would like to have us on TV again, especially since the report on '20/20' made us look so bad."

The door buzzed open. I had nothing to say—I hadn't seen that report—so I walked out.

Last there came a call from a television executive. He needed to be in Little Rock soon, he said, and he hoped to talk with me. Immediately suspicious—no one ever *needs* to be in Little Rock—I still accepted his offer, knowing Rochelle, my mother and brother—perhaps even my father and his new wife, Brooke—would learn of it, and browbeat me if I didn't at least discover what the man had to say. I was instructed to arrive at a penthouse suite at the Peabody, and there was greeted by a familiar-looking man. Suave, tanned, darker even than I, he wore a blue blazer. His gray slacks and salt-and-pepper hair displayed the signs of a recent pressing. His shoes had been shined to a glossy sheen and his firm but not crushing handshake left on my fingers an oily and fragrant film. One hand on my back, the executive escorted me to a seat on a plush sofa, while with the other hand he gestured at the impressive view of North Little Rock and the Arkansas River through the suite's floor to ceiling windows. After asking me if I wanted a drink—I refused—he fixed himself one, talking about how much he enjoyed any chance to visit any of what LA types called the flyover states. Here, he said, fishing for ice cubes with tongs, one got a chance to breath genuine air, of a type that wasn't perfumed with greed and cynicism, and to be among real people. Salt of the earth, I believe he insisted. I asked if this was his first trip to Arkansas and he said, "No, been here dozens of times. I love it. The history, the natural beauty. Ah, the Volunteer State."

I overlooked his error, as his mellow and smooth voice gave a note of authenticity to every word he uttered. Indeed, everything about him—from his graceful movement to the soft peak of his pocket square— suggested he never spent a moment feeling insecure or doubtful he'd not get precisely what he wanted at the rate he dictated. I was sweating and cursing silently the ineffective anti-perspirant I'd bought on sale a week before, when he sat down across from me, holding in both hands a crystal glass filled with amber liquid and ice. "Afraid you were told a little fib," he said. "We hope you're inclined to forgive. But our only business in Arkansas is you." His eyebrows slanted together, then loosened and sprang in curves above his eyes. "No hard feelings?" he said. "We really want to talk to you."

I made a note to joke with Rochelle about the executive's use of the royal we, then thought better of it, wincing as if she'd already adopted that affectation. "Why would you want to talk to me?" I said.

The executive sipped his drink. He hadn't a wrinkle on his clothes or his skin. I believed I'd have to touch my nose against his to discern a pore. "You must know by now you're the only person who still hasn't been on TV yet," he said. "We're here to determine why that is, see if there's anything you'd like to do about that."

"I've been thinking about that," I said. I had. So many people had told me this, beyond my relatives and girlfriend. Rare was the day when someone in the checkout stand or at the bar told me I needed to join the crowd, and for that matter I'd be perfect on some such show or other, their titles as foreign to me as dental hygiene and manners appeared to most of my interlocutors. But I was skeptical of the claim itself. I said to the executive, "Certainly, the number of babies born each day cancels that out."

"We're working on that," he said, "'Welcome to the Real World' is a pilot we're kicking around. Camcorders to every expectant couple and their OB-GYN, that sort of thing. But put it this way, you are, as of this moment, the only person over the age of six who hasn't appeared."

All my life I'd been used to solitude and alienation, but after hearing of my extreme isolation from the crowd, I felt I'd been in constant violation of a fundamental American principle. As the air conditioner clicked on in the suite, I shuddered. "You've been on, as well?" I said, wondering if that's why he seemed someone I knew.

"Sure," he said, "but that's ancient history." The executive moved in closer, his hairless hands no longer holding a drink, but gripped together between his widespread knees, his smile managing to remain while he formed every word. "This is what we want to know. Just what is it that's kept you off the screen?"

I shook my head and shrugged. I didn't know. And that was all I could say: "I don't know."

"You've never been asked on the street for an opinion? Never made faces behind a reporter on location? Don't you like TV?"

I opened my mouth, but he waved me silent. "Before you answer that, you should know many of the people who now appear on some of our finest programs were once the most committed TV-Phobes. They thought it was phony, vulgar, too commercial, empty of social significance. And anyone thinking about the programming of, say, ten years ago, would be absolutely correct. It was a wasteland. Yet look at what we're doing now. Have you seen 'Critical Thinkers of Our Day?' A wonderful panel show featuring our brightest and most attractive unmarried scholars under thirty-five. And what about our documentaries? The series on fraud in the film and recording industries is sure to get us a Peabody. Or at least a People's Choice."

His persuasive powers, I must say, were something to behold. Since the first phone call, I'd expected him to be glib. Never would I have believed, though, I'd be leaning forward in my seat, eager to hear more. I knew of the shows he mentioned. My eyes had been open when they were on, greedily devoured by Rachelle, but in truth I had never paid enough attention to determine quality, either way. "I'm not the biggest TV watcher," I finally said.

The executive sat up as if lifted by invisible wires. After walking around the sofa twice, he said, "Fair enough. Smart guy like you doesn't let his life revolve around the *TV Guide*." He paused. As he'd extended his walking circle behind the couch I was sitting on, I'd lost track of him. So to suddenly see his face near enough to smell his cologne made me fall backward onto the cushioned sofa. "And," he continued, "a certain somebody named Rochelle keeps you entertained."

A foolish grin trembled on my lips, but the executive had already started walking again, now silent, as if awaiting my response. I had nothing to say, no salty aphorism describing how good in bed Rochelle was. His statement reminded me of the effort of being with her, hearing daily how close she was to breaking through and her need to keep the TV on constantly, lest she miss one tip or call for auditions. I wasn't thinking of breaking up then, but if I came home and found a goodbye note, I wouldn't have run out into the street calling her name in anguish, tears streaming down my face.

The executive didn't have as much tolerance for dead air as I. After hanging his blazer neatly on the back of a chair, he said, "So, what do we have to do to get you on a TV show? What could we put together for you?"

His cadences amused me, and I tried to remember what show he'd been on. But it was hard going, as I'd never been one to stare at the screen long enough to remember the stars, let alone the also-rans. The executive continued. "Talk show? Sketch comedy? You're not much of a sports guy, are you? News anchor? What?"

I leaned back in the sofa, recalling whirling lights and shrieking female voices, while the executive moved closer. "How about a documentary? How it feels to be you? Twenty-four hours in the life of? No, no. I've got it. You're a musician, right? Guitar?" He noodled the fingers of his left hand on an imaginary fretboard. I nodded. "So get this," he said. An old fashioned talent show. But it's rigged. You win and keep coming back week after week. As long as you want. Don't worry about the Feds, they're looking the other way all the time now."

"Why me?" I said, my throat a little dry from inactivity. The executive made conversation very easy, as he did the speaking for both of us. But now his confident features slackened. If he experienced any uncertainty, the period was brief. "Because you're our guy," he said. "The man of the moment. And I do emphasize moment." He snapped his fingers. "It's go, go, go. Who knows, in two days everyone's forgotten you and a Boston Terrier who can bark the national anthem has everyone's attention."

"But," I said, "I am the only one who hasn't been on. You said that yourself."

"Comebacks, my friend. Happen all the time. That homeless guy out there who was on the news program about the underclass? He cleans up, gets a haircut and a new suit, boom, he's on every Sunday telling you how to be just like him."

"I suppose."

He was stooped directly in front of me now. At last I could see the pores on his elegant nose. A few beads of sweat formed near his graying temples. "So what do you say?" he said. "We've laid out a bunch of options. Which suits you best?"

Now I remembered: he'd been the host of a mid-morning game show, opposite of Bob Barker, and my mother only watched when the *Price is Right* was a repeat. In the last months of its single season, he dressed up in all manner of costumes, and I could recall his smile straining beneath a hobo's greasepaint beard. I chewed the inside of my lower lip, wondering whether I should pretend to mull over his requests. But I did not want to get the executive's hopes up or laugh in his face. Besides, I was booked at the guitar shop for a beginner's class that I knew would start with questions on how to set your instrument aflame. I put my palms on my thighs and pushed myself up. "I'm sorry," I said. "I'm not your man."

"Why?" He stood, clutching his side as if my words had wounded him.

I shrugged.

The executive strode toward the door. Beads of sweat slipped down his face, leaving skinny tracks a shade lighter than his bronze complexion. "You know," he said, "a lot of times a guy who doesn't follow trends thinks because of that he's in the right. Marching to the beat of a different drum, you know. But I'll tell you, sometimes that guy is wrong. Dead wrong. He thinks those who're following the crowd live unhappy lives while he's like that Thoreau guy, up in Vermont."

"Massachusetts," I corrected. "The Bay State."

"Whatever. But did he really have a good time in life? Was his, what, integrity worth it? You tell me? Because the people out there aren't stupid. Not by a long stretch. At some point, when you're the one out of step, you've got to ask, are they all wrong? Three hundred million men, women and children?"

"I'm not your man," I said.

His hands, suddenly clenched, shook between us. "You mean you won't give up your integrity even if it keeps you out of step with the rest of the nation?"

There was that word again, integrity. Truth was, though, I didn't have any more integrity than this blow-dried, cosmetically-altered failure of a game show host before me. In fact, I was a petty, selfish man who delighted in the foibles of others because it kept me from having to acknowledge my own. No wonder I enjoyed the company of Rochelle and visited my brother regularly. No wonder indeed I wasn't making a therapist rich, whining about my parents' divorce. All these people in my life kept me amused—far better than any TV show, fact or fiction— and I didn't give them any emotional connection or genuine affection. But, like the executive, they ascribed to me a kind of moral superiority that I knew would be lost the moment my made up face materialized on the flat screens of theirs and countless Americans. Give that up? Not for the executive's petty promises.

To him, I shrugged again, then stepped toward the door, out of his reach. When I turned the door knob, he tried again. "Anything you want. Just tell us. We want you on the air."

"Sorry," I said and stepped into the hall.

"Fine then," the executive said, dusting his soft hands together. "You know, we don't need your permission. Any day now, our lobbyists are going to remove all that blessed need for privacy and we'll be able to shoot anyone, anytime. Won't need a stupid waiver anymore."

"Ok," I said, leaving him behind.

"You'll be on," he shouted. "One day. Believe me!"

And I almost made it down to the lobby without a stab of regret. One of the many seeds tossed by the executive germinated, and I feared I'd turned down an important opportunity. What if I were wrong? Had I lost my one chance? My hand rose shakily and my index finger hovered near the button for the top floor. But then the door opened, and into the car walked a man who'd appeared as a young Frank Sinatra on "And We Sing Like Them Too," which was Rochelle's second or third favorite show, as she believed she was a nose job away from resembling Mariah Carey. Then, behind the concierge desk, I saw a woman who'd brought an oil painting to one of the antique appraisal shows my mother loved. She left knowing her "family heirloom" was worth little more than the canvas. And then, coming through the front doors, a pair of octogenarian identical twins, whom I'd read about in the paper. Their true-life story of separation and reconciliation had won three Emmy's, though now they were each suing the producers for more money, as well as their wives for divorce—also twins, but fraternal—and appearing often on *The Trials of Celebrity*. All, though, were looking more at me than I at them, each with that gaze suggesting their minds busy at work trying to determine just why they were having trouble placing me. Being neither clearly black or white,

I'd seen that gaze all my life, but this afternoon I knew it was different. "Are you on or off?" the young Frank Sinatra drawled.

I smiled and jumped out of the elevator before the doors closed, knowing I might be caught off-guard by some guerilla camcorder tactics or Barbara Walters would eventually interview me and I'd have a great story for why it'd taken so long for me to appear. (I'd even play for her my guitar!) It was inevitable, my joining the television ranks, but I could wait it out. For now I knew I was the most famous man in these United States, and I was just starting to enjoy myself.

Ethnic Studies

Naked, save for white towels around our waists, we march down the cool, quiet hall. Without a word, our steps have fallen into a cadence as orderly as a chain gang's. The tile's cold and gritty beneath our feet. My feet, I should say, as I don't want to assume my experience mirrors that of the three other men. From the rear of the line, I watch Dr. Pruitt, a balding bantamweight with an MFA and Ph.D. from Illinois State, moving alongside Teng Lo and Amos Talking Stone. He jogs to keep up, but his stubby red ponytail doesn't bounce. I'd suggest a visit to the barber, but I'm sure the tail reminds him of the early seventies, an era he reeks of today: sandalwood, unwashed armpits, tofu belches, and a meager but pungent tang of Thai Stick. "Some of them have never seen a person of color in the flesh before," he's saying. Around me, I note closed classroom doors, beige walls, the blunt, black hands of an institutional clock. No one in line speaks. We keep moving until we reach the end of the hall, where an open door beckons.

"In here," Dr. Pruitt says, breathing a little heavily through his sharp nose. Last night, at dinner, and again this afternoon, he begged us to call him Kyle. Ten years out of college, I respect titles as much as I did when I was eighteen and eager for A's.

We enter, remaining in step until Javier Montoya, our unofficial leader, halts. Amos Talking Stone, Teng Lo and I come to a rest facing the wall opposite from where we entered. None of the expected fifty-five students speaks, though chairs groan, clothes rustle, and stomachs gurgle in anticipation of lunch. In my head I hear again the enthusiastic words of Dr. Pruitt. "This is such a wonderful opportunity for all of us. If you guys just be yourselves, I'm sure everything will work out fine." He told us this only moments before, when we were in his office, shedding clothes and concealing privates as best we could with the starched towels. As for what's now going through the minds of Javier, Teng and Amos, I can't be sure. I do have a pretty good idea, though.

Through a streaked window, I stare at the flat, grassy plains of the campus. According to Dr. Pruitt, it was farmland only thirty years ago, but I wouldn't say they've made much improvement. I shift my eyes to Teng, who's considerably shorter, almost a foot. He's got a head full of well combed and glossy black hair, and his skin's several shades lighter than mine. Still, he, Javier and Amos and I are all in the general family of brown. Reflecting on this, I forget for a moment where I am, then the door slams with a dramatic finality. Dr. Pruitt signals us with an open palm, and we four turn to face the students. In a glimpse, I know this afternoon's objective sounds as likely as Minister Farrakhan attending a seder. That fifty-five underclassmen, drawn from farms, small towns and the suburbs of this state's one metropolis, will somehow gain from us an insight into the various races we are? Who's kidding who? Dr. Pruitt won't even say "race." It's an artificial construct, he claims. He prefers "ethnicity." Now he introduces us, and for once I'm glad my last name is Stearns, because it's the only one he doesn't feel the need to adopt an accent for. When he says "Montoya" he sounds like a bad mix of Desi Arnaz and Ricardo Montalban. For now I shut my eyes. My head tilts back. And, like a nervous patient, I await the physician's intrusive and inevitable touch.

A man's got to eat. And no one's hungrier than a black actor with no theatrical roles in two years, fifty consecutive unsuccessful commercial auditions, and lately reduced to singing, in the garb and timbre of Nat King Cole, "Mona Lisa" to a roomful of octogenarians. When I saw Dr. Pruitt's advertisement, tacked up between fliers for babysitters and used Soloflexes on the bulletin board of the Southside Community Players, I was first drawn to the headline requesting ETHNIC MINORITIES AT EASE IN FRONT OF CROWDS. Then I viewed the facts pertinent to my mean condition: 500 dollar appearance fee, free transportation, meals and lodging for two nights. Had the number inked on my palm and was dialing it, toll-free, on the pay phone down the hall, certain I'd be getting in touch too late to capitalize.

Obviously, I didn't read the whole ad. Didn't take note of the means by which Dr. Pruitt had come up with the cash. (An alum had published a salacious novel about comely coeds, priapic professors, and the various usages of the Humanities Lounge. He donated a slice of his royalties to the school, to dispense however they chose.) Nor would I concern myself with the conditions spelled out in the letter of agreement, that, much to my surprise, arrived in the mail two days after I'd left my name and number on the answering machine. It was like, Yeah, yeah, yeah, performance in accord with instructor's wishes, fee to be paid only after conclusion of service . . . . What mattered was that some third-rate state university was going to take care of yours truly for playing a role I'd been practicing all my life: the black man. I hit Kinko's so fast, when I faxed in the agreement, the ink of my signature was still damp.

But I wasn't alone in my ignorance. My fellow models hadn't paid much attention to those other details, I'd learn. Yesterday, we all arrived at the tiny local airport around six. Given the monochromatic background of faces, it was easy to pick each other out, and we were making introductions at the baggage carrousel by the time Dr. Pruitt showed. He then drove us in a university van to a chain Mexican restaurant, where Javier, a thin and intense Chicano with gray eyes from Des Plaines, stared angrily at the tacky piñatas, papier-mâché burros and the pitcher of frozen margaritas on each table. As at the airport, I got the vibe most persons of color feels after walking into a previously all-white establishment, but I decided tonight, with my immediate company, I'd ignore it, maybe even enjoy myself. Once the startled-looking waitress took our orders and Dr. Pruitt excused himself to make a call, we four got to rapping, and discovered we were all over thirty, poor, unmarried and overeducated— five graduate degrees between us. (Javier had a Masters in Poli Sci along with his JD.) As well, no one was sure what might happen next in his life, which made the five hundred a hard fee to pass up.

Teng Lo had flown in from Dallas, his home of the past fifteen years, but he was originally from a small village in South Vietnam, one of two siblings from his six who survived the journey to the States. He welded bumpers and shopping carts into what he called "arrangements" that represented "the makings of post-millennial America," but he was thinking about going into full time housepainting, as the last five galleries that displayed his work closed shortly after those exhibits.

Amos was Anishanaabe, living in his hometown of St. Paul and enrolled at the White Earth Res. Though he'd graduated from the Iowa Writer's Workshop, he hadn't published a lick since two years ago, when, as he put it, "A Hallmark card appeared in Unread Review." Carpentry paid his rent in the warm months, but the long winters could be awfully lean. He kept his graying hair in a braided ponytail that reached the middle of his back (shaming Dr. Pruitt's stub) and he knew some of the folk who fought the good fight for little pay with Javier at Westside Legal Services.

We were an interesting bunch, but no one had a clear idea—beyond the check at the end—what we were expected to do here. Amos thought it was a Q & A with the faculty and had his opening remarks typed on a stack of index cards as thick as a poker deck. Teng agreed with the Q & A part, but swore we'd be meeting students, whom he was prepared to correct when they asked him about being Chinese. Javier, like Amos, had prepared remarks—a single spaced, five page screed about white privilege—but, like me, he didn't know to which audience he would give it. As we pondered this, Dr. Pruitt returned to his seat at the end of the table. I noticed a blue smudge on the side of his nose. Overall, his features were as soft and drooping as an aging cherub's, but his nose, long and sharp as an ax-blade, stood out from the rest. "Got some schmutz there, Dr. Pruitt," I said, gesturing toward his face.

"Kyle," he said. "Thought I washed that off at the studio." He wet his napkin in his water glass, then vigorously scrubbed until his nose was pinker and free of the colorful stain.

"Got it," I said, smiling as I did after answering correctly in class.

Teng ground out a Vantage, saying, "What kind of studio is it, Kyle?"

"Nothing much, just the one on campus."

"Thought you were Art History?" Amos said.

"A little of both." Dr. Pruitt smiled shyly and closed his eyes. Our waitress, her eyes and mouth still wide open, dropped off a margarita in front of the good professor, then backed away.

Teng said, "What's your medium?"

"Acrylics. Oils. I try to cover it all."

"Exhibited anywhere?" Teng said, reaching for another Vantage.

"I used to, but that was back when, you know, art seemed to really matter. Politically, I mean. Back when lives were changed for the good every day. Man, you guys should have seen it."

Then it hit me, just as Dr. Pruitt was wrapping up his homily to times past. I looked at my newly-met peers, knowing full well why we were here and what we had to do. Outraged, I wanted to shout "No fucking way," and storm off like Al Sharpton. Then I remembered my checking account and the bills due in less than a week I stayed put. Yes, we only had to be "at ease in front of a crowd," but do so in front of Dr. Pruitt's Life Drawing class, made up of many who'd never seen people like us outside TV screens. I said this aloud, and Amos laughed so hard he started to choke. Javier thumped him on his broad back and said, "You've got to be kidding. He's kidding, right?" And about the time Amos was exhaling, Teng lit his Vantage, Dr. Pruitt dipped his nose into a slushy red margarita, and both shook their heads.

So we stand in this chilly room, the focus of so many sets of wide, white eyes. Few students have put charcoal to canvas yet. The class breaks down to about sixty percent females, but they and their male cohorts just stare, look at one another, then stare some more. I wish the four of us could execute some ruse—like dropping our towels and mooning these kids—that would allow us to keep the money and make this hour less onerous, but I haven't spoken to anyone since dinner. Before dropping us off at four different motels, Dr. Pruitt showed more of the agreement's fine print—the reason no close-reading Negroes had followed me here—and it specified we were not to contact each other between our arrival and performance, revealing how much Dr. Pruitt and his gang had thought these shenanigans through. Last night, locked away in my room, I wondered if they ever worried they wouldn't get models. Teng, Javier, Amos, and I: we're four smart fellows, and we fell like laundry down a chute. Did vanity bring us here? Or the fee? And what did either answer say about us?

In the back of the classroom, Dr. Pruitt says, "I can feel a lot of energy in this room. I don't know if it's positive or negative. But it's here, it's palpable." Next to me, Teng coughs, a pleasant diversion from the pervading nonsense. In the front row, a pair of blonde girls giggle, then duck behind their easels. A flabby jock in a ball cap and stained sweats stares at me as if to see who'll blink first. Amos whispers, "I want to say 'boo.'" Teng nods, his slim fingers twitching without a smoke between them.

Out of the side of his mouth, Javier says, "Can he hear us? Pruitt?"

"Maybe," I say. I watch the professor walk up to one of the few brunettes in class. He places his hand on her easel and gestures broadly. "Open yourself up to the possibilities. What story might each man's eyes tell?" he says, hammy as a high school play.

As if on their own, my eyes shut. In graduate school, I delivered strip-o-grams for two months, but the near nudity of that job didn't bother me as much as today's exposure. Then, even in Speedos, I was playing a role. Today, I'm just as naked, but far more vulnerable. I'm me. And though I doubt any of the "artists" could capture the neuroses, flaws, and short-comings that I feel are as obvious as my ashy elbows and knees, I know they're on display.

So I promise this is the last time I'll debase myself, that things won't get any worse today. Then the door opens and a portly fellow in beige corduroys and a brown sweater rushes forward. He slaps at a sheaf of milky blond hair that flies from his pink dome until he stands before Dr. Pruitt, who says, "Milt. What brings you here?"

The two shake hands with big pumps and friendly touches to the elbow. I check out my pals: Teng looks sleepy and small as a child. Amos smirks and cracks the knuckles of his large, carpenter's hands. Skinny as he is, Javier looks ready to hurt someone. The cords in his long neck twitch and his eyelids flutter. As if aware I'm looking, he turns to me, his eye color shifting to a steely hue. He mouths the words, "Who is that?" I shrug, turn back to the door, open a crack. In the narrow space I can see the pantlegs and shuffling shoes of more than a few people. None is moving very fast, as if all are waiting for the next class in this room to begin. Dr. Pruitt shouts, "What a great idea," and the other fellow—a professor, I presume—jogs back to the door. On opening it, a horde of students stream in. Every minority on campus must be at basketball practice or the Diversity Center, because I don't see one person of color now fighting for space between the first row of easels and us.

"Artists," Dr. Pruitt says, rubbing his finger against his nose. "Dr. Jansen has brought his American History II class to join us. Now we'll have our models' psyches and physiques at once!"

"That's not part of the deal, Kyle," Javier says, and he's hot. He steps out of line toward where Drs. Pruitt and Jansen stand, but too many students are getting seated between him and them. "That's not part of the deal," he says again. Meanwhile, Amos, a few inches shorter than Javier, but twice his weight, grabs him by the arm. Teng whispers, "Five hundred, man. Just take it easy." Under my breath, I mention that our clothes are still in Dr. Pruitt's office and he's got the keys. "Few more minutes," I say. "You want to get out of that towel, don't you?"

"I want to get out of this room," he whispers harshly. We look toward the door in time to see Dr. Pruitt, as if in response to Javier, shutting it. His nose, sharp as a hawk's beak, dominates his face as he walks toward us, saying, "I'm afraid it is, though not explicitly."

"Huh?" Amos says.

"The agreement," he says curtly. "You agreed to perform according to the instructor's wishes." He pauses, and suddenly he's no longer the harmless art professor. Like the manager of a strip club, he eyes us up and down, making sure we're prepared to satisfy the audience's every whim. He says, "And, well, though I know it's fairly impromptu, it's my wish that you answer some questions."

Behind him stands the portly Jansen, grinning and rubbing his hands like a malevolent child. "We just got into the sixties and the protest movement. They're a really good group of kids," he says. "Inquisitive and willing to learn about other cultures."

"*Other* cultures," Amos says, shaking his head. We're more or less back in line, though it's not as straight as it was and Javier won't look up from the floor. While I'm certain the position of being the only Indian/Asian/ Latino/Black in a classroom isn't new to any of us, I feel the gut-clench of difference and the increasing heat of eyes on my skin. Both professors now step away, and Jansen says, "Class, our guests welcome your questions." He props his hands contentedly on his fat stomach, leans against the wall.

Pruitt walks toward Jansen, saying, "Artists, stay focused. You're about to see the souls of these men."

"Man, he's been talking that shit all day, " Teng mumbles, and all of us nod. I doubt any student here could get our skin colors correct, let alone capture our essences. All depictions of me, I suspect, will resemble police sketches of suspected gang-bangers from Cabrini-Green.

Of the students closest to us, most scribble in their notebooks and try not to look our way. I can't blame them for being shy—we are nearly naked—but a few, mostly males with Greek lettering somewhere on their person, smile like a party of planters in 1810 New Orleans. A blond volunteer raises his hand, then says, "Are you all *from* America?"

In line we look at one another. I'm unsure who should field that, or if we all should reply. Amos might remind the boy how his people were here first. Javier, no doubt, would point out that it's Americas, and the U.S. is only part of them. In the end, Teng goes it alone, saying, "I'm from South Vietnam originally." We scuff our naked soles against the floor and wait.

The next questioner, a girl with close-cropped hair and a nosering, wearing tattered and scribbled-on jeans, says, "Have you felt out of place on campus?" She scowls at her classmates, indicating the question's more rhetorical than anything else, and that she's down with us. Teng mumbles something about warm hospitality, and Amos says he hasn't been asked to do a rain dance. Javier and I remain silent, though judging from the twitching fists that hang at his sides, he's not merely counting down the seconds.

Just then, Dr. Jansen pushes himself forward from the wall. He slaps at the thin hair on top of his head—he and Dr. Pruitt would be better off with a baldhead, like me—then says, "Good questions, both. But we might try to relate some of our questions to the issues we were discussing from our textbook, in the sections titled, 'Let Freedom Ring' and 'You Say You Want a Revolution.' Anyone?"

No hands go up. Dr. Pruitt reminds his students to view us deeply, but I doubt he wants realistic portrayals of our livers, lungs and bowels. My internal clock tells me, at best, fifteen minutes remain, which might go faster if we get a decent question, one that Javier could filibuster to with pages from his prepared remarks. Only I don't know that any question devised by these kids is one I—or any of my partners—want to answer.

After a minute or two more of silence and eyes that look up briefly then swiftly shut or turn to sneakers, one boy stands, smooths his hand over his light brown hair. He's got that look of cocky certainty I've never seen in my mirror, and an Abercrombie and Fitch wardrobe fresh off the shelves. He smiles, digs a hand in the back pocket of his jeans. Maybe a little Irish blood flows in his WASP-y veins, but not enough to keep his family off the Society page. I'm willing him to ask Javier about illegal aliens stealing jobs from hard-working Americans. Only I'm sure he's looking right at me. "What makes blacks and whites so different?" he says with a smirk, as if to tell all his cronies he already knows the answer, just wants to hear what the nigger has to say. For a moment, my eyes fall upon his, then I turn my gaze to the fellows in line: no one looks anything but depressed. Who can blame them? Five hundred dollars doesn't seem as large a number as it did before. It might pay some bills, but not enough to make up for the indignities of the hour. I don't think any of us are scheduling a return for next semester.

But I've still got this question to contend with, and the race man in me is shaping a reply, about how I'm not a representative of all black folks, that we're a people made up of as many different types as you can find in any race. Or ethnicity. Another voice inside whispers I should tell this punk to sit his ass down before it gets kicked. For the most part, I want to stay silent, keep my lips clamped together, but Dr. Pruitt's demand still lingers: Perform according to the instructor's wishes. An interesting word, perform. Though obviously relevant to me as an actor, it doesn't fit only on the stage. A smile slips up on me as I consider my answer. The kid stands again. "What makes you guys so different from whites?" he asks, louder this time.

"Go on ask your girlfriend, jack. She could tell you a whole lot," I say, with just enough of a pelvic thrust to make the bottom of my towel dance. And I am no longer vain or gullible, a broke, black actor too sensitive for words, I am every stylish Player that ever stepped out of a Cadillac as long as a city block. I am superbad, got it goin on and on and on. It's a role I've never played, in life or on stage, but tonight it seems like the finest set of threads on the rack, and feels so good on my skin.

Poor Teng looks up at me as if I dropped the towel. Amos, with a nod and a genuine grin, turns to the students and removes the rubber band from his ponytail, shakes out his hair so it hangs on both sides of his face. "Heap good question," he says, rolling his well-defined shoulders. "Red man think your girlfriend like bareback ride with him, too."

The questioner appears beaten. His mouth can't shut and he blinks as if punched in the nose. Slowly, one hand gropes toward the floor and the rest of him follows. At once, Drs. Pruitt and Jansen move forward, but do so slowly, as if uncertain the ground between us is secure.

"Um, gentleman," Dr. Pruitt says.

The students have all dropped their writing instruments, including the artists, who've moved away from their easels and now wander forward, as if I just made an altar call. Dr. Pruitt walks close enough for me to smell his foul hippie self. "Um, guys," he stammers. "What do you think you're doing?"

"Getting paid, *ese*," Javier says. "Ain't that right, homes?" He reaches behind Teng and Amos, and I slap his open palm. Amos looks as cigar-store as humanly possible. He says, "Wampum good for fire-water. Manitou say so."

"And buy many derishus dogs for eating," Teng says, as if he read it off a fortune cookie.

A few students are laughing—the woman with the nosering, for one—but most look to their professors, waiting for some suggestion or order that will make sense of this development. Pruitt steps toward me, then backtracks, calls for his students to get behind their easels. Jansen wipes his pink mitt over his forehead, worrying the few hairs left. Pruitt whispers, "This is turning into a farce. You're making a big mistake."

"Turning into?" Javier says, his pachuco voice gone, but the volume still high. "It was a farce to begin with, Kyle."

Pruitt doesn't know what to say to that. He rubs his nose and slumps, while, behind him, Jansen says, "Should I dismiss both classes?"

"That might be the best thing. We can't let this go on any longer."

"I thought this is what you wanted, Kyle," Teng says. "We're just being ourselves." He reaches beneath his towel and retrieves from it a Vantage and a wooden match. His thumbnail raises a flare from the matchhead, then he fires up his smoke.

"I'll tell them," Jansen says. He turns to the students, wiping at his forehead and saying, "Um, I know that we're a little early for a conclusion. Ten minutes, you know, but." He turns and looks at us. Pruitt's scowling—his face growing as red as his hair—and nodding at Jansen. Jansen says, "As I said, we're a little early, but it seems for the best that we say goodbye to our guests. Sorry it didn't work out as we hoped. These gentleman apparently decided to make fun of us."

Now I realize I have at least one more thing to say.

I can't let these two turn this around on us. And before Jansen can say another word, I step forward—that is, I *slide* forward, Superfly smooth—and get so close to them that Jansen, frightened, smacks Pruitt in the face with a flailing hand. Grabbing his nose, Pruitt slumps away, moaning, and Jansen follows, saying, "Are you all right?" This puts me alone on center stage. I know each line I need. I say, "All y'all are just too stiff. Loosen up! Axin all these questions. Starin like we ain't flesh and blood mens. Don't you want to get to know us like folks?" Teng's smoke curls my way, and I turn, give the fellows the thumbs up. Don't worry, y'all. I know what I'm doing. "Tell you what the real problem is," I say. "Look at what you wearin, compared to what we got on. Somebody ain't playin fair, and it ain't the fellas in the towels. You want to find out some stuff, I suggest you even up the sides. Shuck them duds and we'll be right on time."

Next sound I hear is applause, coming from Javier and Teng. They each break from the line, head toward a different section of the room. "*Es verdad*," Javier says. "These coats and jeans are confining, *chicos y chicas*. Let's get down to the real, let's get down to some skin." Teng inhales, blows smoke rings and smiles, as Amos takes up a place in front of the door. He shakes his head at Jansen and Pruitt, crosses his thick arms over his wide chest. "No one leave or enter unless they know password," he says. "How."

"What you people got to say then?" I say.

And though it takes a minute, some students stand. Our friend with the nosering tosses away her shredded jeans jacket as a pair of brunettes unbuttons their smocks. A smiling blond steps out of her shoes. Even one of the fellows, the beefy jock who stared me down earlier, waves his cap and his socks above his head, and says, "Take it off!'

I look at Pruitt and Jansen, hunched together in a

corner, harmless. I tip an imaginary cap at them, then turn to the students. Another two or three are tugging at belts or shoe laces. The shyer ones unzip their coats. Most everyone appears to at least think about it, looking at us, then to their peers as if to see how far to go. At the front of the room, I look on, a man at ease for the first time in a long while. "That's right," I say in a voice entirely my own. "Now we can begin."

The Lessons of Effacement

On the sidewalk, after another Monday at the office, Jerome glanced over his shoulder. Behind him, he spied again among pedestrians the figure in a trench coat. Though it was a mild April day, the figure's collar was up and the same houndstooth hat bobbed above. Jerome sped up, contorting his body so as not to trod on the heels of others. Again, he looked for this person trailing him, and as had been the case for the past seven weekdays—how many before that, Jerome wondered— the figure paused, as if he knew he'd been spotted, and fell back in the crowd. After a few seconds, though, he resumed following Jerome, maintaining a distance of no fewer than twenty feet.

Things were going according to Jerome's plans, which disappointed as much as it excited him. He'd hoped to discover these sightings were the sort of urban events that threatened peril at first, then, after closer inspection, turned out to be coincidences. Now he hesitated, wiped his damp mustache with his fingers and thumb, measuring how much further he had to go before reaching the alley between the shoeshine stand and the barbershop. Less than a full two blocks, he figured, allowing his stride to lengthen. He was very nearly running, his striped necktie bouncing off his shirtfront, by the time he ducked in the alley. As he expected, he found a space of at least five feet between some trashcans and fitted himself into that niche, pressing his palms and back against the rough brick of the shoeshine stand's exterior wall. A few gulps of air steadied his breathing. If things continued as he'd planned, the person in the trench coat would stop here, try to gauge in which direction Jerome had headed. And if the person proved to be as small as he had judged, Jerome would trap the stranger's arms against his sides, then steer the both of them across the street into the Excello Lounge, where he would find out what the hell was going on. All this attention baffled him. Why wouldn't it? When your only offenses in life were drinking out of the juice carton and being born black in these United States, what could warrant such certain persecution?

As still as he was, his pulse throbbed in his neck, while at the base of his stomach a chill feeling spread, heralding panic or anticipation. A number of folk walked past, none of them noticing him in the gathering shadows. Jerome wondered from where he had summoned this courage and cunning. It was unlike him to hide between rusting and battered garbage cans. This was more the behavior of a character in the movies and novels he loved, those double-dealing detectives whose exploits he enjoyed during weekends in his apartment. Eating Twizzlers, microwave popcorn, and drinking Cherry Cokes, he overlooked the fact that most blacks who appeared carried drinks to the heroes or carted the heroine's luggage. In life—where he worked for the electric company in public relations—he'd done nothing to prepare for the excitements faced by Philip Marlowe or John Shaft. That was why he'd given himself the opportunity to measure the stranger before he acted. Though the person might be shorter, he could be solid as a fireplug, and Jerome, who couldn't bench press the bar without a spotter, didn't want to proceed rashly, then regret the subsequent bruises. Yet he wanted more than an answer to this curious phenomenon. He wanted an end. Blowing warm air on his hands, he tensed his knees, convincing himself he was ready to strike.

That's when he saw him. Alone, his back to the narrow alley, the stranger paused, and the hat moved right to left. Jerome pounced, relieved to find he was at least six inches taller. Even more grateful to grab the stranger's skinny wrist, he pushed him to the crosswalk. After waiting for the lights to change, Jerome double-timed toward the Excello. The stranger whimpered hoarsely. "Be quiet," Jerome hissed. Inside the smoky confines of the Excello—a tavern Jerome passed every day but, a teetotaler, had never entered—he found a booth in the far left corner, dumped the stranger in one side, then debated whether to sit across from or next to his accoster. Across might look more commonplace to the other patrons but might allow the stranger an opportunity to escape. A glance at the bar and the tables, however, showed only a few customers, none of whom looked in any direction but toward his glass. Jerome fitted himself into the same side of the booth. Skimming over the vinyl seat, he bumped his hip into the soft flank of the stranger, who whimpered again.

"Ok," Jerome said. "Hats off."

Huddled against the wall, the stranger lifted one arm as if to ward off an imminent blow from Jerome, who'd been in two fights in his life: one with his older brother Terence—a draw; the other with dark-skinned LaTonya Graves, who, in the words of the other fifth graders, wore Jerome's narrow ass *out*. "Can I talk now?" the cringing figure stammered.

"Not yet," Jerome said. A tall, white bartender with a stern gray crewcut appeared at the booth. He dealt two coasters and sighed, "What can I get you?"

Marlowe or Shaft would order a bourbon, but Jerome was thirsty from effort as well as excitement and fear. "Iced tea," he said, his elbow sinking into the side of the stranger. "Two iced teas," he said.

The bartender hobbled away as one with sore feet. Jerome turned, saw the houndstooth hat—garish and oversized, the very thing that tipped him off to the stranger's presence. "I said take off your hat," Jerome said, trying to put a growl behind his words but sounding more like a man needing to spit.

Trembling, the stranger's gloved hands removed the hat. Jerome watched him place it on the table, then viewed the top of the man's head. The close cropped black curls startled Jerome. He felt he was looking at his own head. "Turn and face me," he said.

"Can I say something?" the stranger said.

"Turn and face me first."

While planning, Jerome had imagined this moment but never saw a face, only a blank, which at the time seemed evidence of his confusion. Who would want to follow him? Now he saw a black man's face, noting directly the man's face was as dark as his gloves, his round eyes streaked with red veins and his chin and upper lip as clean and soft as a woman's. Jerome stroked his mustache, trimmed every other morning to a quarter inch in length. He knew not what to say. For whatever reason, until he saw the stranger's hair, he'd never suspected another black man.

"Here's your tea," Jerome heard from behind.

His grip tightening on the stranger's arm, he turned to the bartender, wondering what the man was thinking. A couple of queers? Jerome wanted him gone. "We'll run a tab," he said.

The bartender walked away.

"Ok to talk yet?"

When Jerome turned, he relaxed his grip. He drank

from his tea. It was bitter, probably from a mix. "Who are you?" he said.

Silence. The stranger ducked his head.

"You can talk now," Jerome said.

The stranger cleared his throat. "Your double," he said.

"My what?"

"Your double. Can I drink some tea?"

Jerome nodded, his mind a blur.

"This is what you drink, right? Iced tea in the evening? I know it's coffee in the morning and afternoon."

Eyes opened wide, Jerome said, "Why do you want to know?"

"I need to do everything you do. Exactly how you do it. Like I said, I'm your double."

"You're serious?"

The stranger studied how Jerome held his glass, then mimicked the splay of his fingers. "Very serious," he said. "I want your life."

Jerome leaned back in the booth. He'd read about this phenomenon before. People one day showing up at work or home and finding another behind the desk or slicing the Christmas ham, Xeroxes who'd managed to convince loved ones and peers that they were indeed the real deal. The original often battled his double for primacy and sometimes, Jerome recalled with a shudder, didn't win. Why hadn't he considered such an explanation when he first spotted the houndstooth hat? Because these incidents were rare, for one, confined to the world of the well-heeled and well-bred. And he was Jerome Manning, trained since birth by his parents to be mostly meek and entirely mild, a model minority. Bertha and Marvin Manning wanted their boys to strive for success among whites but stressed to both they were to act in ways that did not disgrace the race. "You can't just do whatever *you* want," Mr. Manning, a CME minister, often preached.

"Think about the others who're going to follow." Thirty years old, Jerome often wondered if he should fashion a path all his own, but never before had he thought someone emulate him. "My life," he said. "Why do you want it?"

Like a butterfly struggling from its chrysalis, the stranger wriggled his shoulders from the coat, revealing the same white shirt, striped tie and dark jacket that Jerome wore. Jerome almost reached for the man but dropped his hands to his thighs. "Regularity," the man said. "People always say variety and spontaneity make life worth living, but deep down what we want to know it's bran for breakfast, tuna on wheat with an apple and an orange at every lunch"

"How did you know," Jerome began, then concluded the seven days of surveillance had been far more complete than he first believed. How else could this stranger know his breakfast cereal and the contents of his brown paper sack? As well, in a perverse way, he felt flattered. No way was he handing over his humdrum existence, but being selected by this would-be double gave him reason to smile. He smoothed his mustache with his finger. "One problem," Jerome said. "You're nothing like me."

"What do you mean?" Though the double looked genuinely hurt, Jerome didn't know where to begin. He was a half-foot taller, with longer arms and thinner fingers. Taut in the midsection where the double was spongy. The double lacked facial hair, which Jerome supposed could be taken care of with time or a costume mustache, but the most glaring dissimilarity was right on the surface. Jerome picked up the man's hand, pushed down the cuff of his jacket and held his arm next to the double's. Jerome's skin color was sandy, tending to yellow. The double's was as deep brown as the shell of a brazil nut. "We don't even look alike," Jerome said.

The double moved his head side to side as though before a mirror. "I think I favor you a lot."

Jerome sighed. "What's your name?"

"Jerome Manning," he said.

"Your real name."

"Jerome Manning, just like my mother Bertha and the Reverend . . . "

Jerome interrupted: "That's enough." After hearing him speak for a while, Jerome detected his own careful cadences, which he'd gained after hours of practice to remove any ethnic shading or tone. Jerome sipped his tea, looked up to see the double mirroring his actions. Simultaneously, they put their glasses down. "I'm not going to persuade you to stop?" Jerome said.

"Too late," the double said. "I can't turn back."

"All right," Jerome said. None of the films or books he loved might supply him with a solution. He'd have to rely on his own experiences, of which there were few. His double did have it right: his life was routine and, Jerome suspected, easily duplicated. But of one thing he was certain: no one who knew Jerome would be fooled by this fellow. He took another glance. They weren't even generally similar. He wanted to say this again but believed the double needed to hear the sentiment from another. He looked around the bar. It was too dark, everyone too deeply drunk. The double needed to hear from someone with clear vision, in the light of day.

"Go to the office tomorrow," Jerome said.

"Of course," the double said, smoothing his jacket sleeves. Jerome looked down at his own sleeves, surprised he was doing the same.

"If you manage to convince everyone you're me, then maybe, maybe, I'll let you take over. Heck, I could use a break from being Jerome." The words sounded ridiculous, yet Jerome knew they needed saying in order to bring about a satisfactory end. The double stuck out a wide, gloved palm. Jerome felt the grip of his slender fingers matched, then shook. "Deal?" the double said, just before Jerome spoke. He looked again at the double. No chance. Not even in the same ballpark. "Deal," he said.

The next morning, in the lobby men's room of his office building, Jerome and his double stood before the bank of mirrors, going over for the last time the procedure to follow. In the hours between their time at the Excello and now, Jerome had grown convinced that the farcical manner of today's events would chase the double out of the building, if not the whole city limits. The double still had a clean upper lip, as well as a slight limp, which he concealed badly, dragging his right foot every few steps. Jerome wanted to learn the cause—perhaps the trauma explained the man's precarious mental condition—but when he asked the double said, "What limp?"

Now, though they were both dressed in khaki suits, light blue shirts and pale green ties with tiny blue paisleys, Jerome saw the double had failed to glean how fanatical his mother had made him about ironing. The double's shirtfront displayed a network of soft wrinkles. The pants bore not even the faintest of creases. "You ready?" Jerome said. The double had tied a sloppy four-in-hand knot. Jerome tightened his single-windsor. Each man looked away from the mirror. They faced each other. "Born ready," the double said.

"What do you do at the first sign of trouble?"

"Come down here and find you."

"Then what?" Jerome brushed imaginary lint off his lapels, as did the double, a second behind. He appeared unused to office wear, fidgeting and worrying his sleeves with his hands. "We go upstairs and tell everyone it's a joke. That I'm your cousin from Peoria and we wanted to have a little fun."

Before they left the Excello, Jerome had added these caveats, thinking not only would they disabuse the double of his delusion but that the explanation might endear Jerome to his coworkers, who he doubted believed their sole black co-worker was capable of a practical joke. To them, he felt sure, he was as inoffensive as a black man could be. He apologized when his shadow touched theirs and laughed hard at the stalest jokes. Moreover, this might be his first step away from his parents' plans for success, a step in a direction toward a life lead for Jerome, not for the next generation of African Americans who prayed he didn't ruin their chances. "Remember," Jerome said. "Steve Bransby calls me Jerry. And Mr. Ealen calls me Gordon sometimes."

The double blinked. "Who's Gordon?"

"Another black guy," Jerome said, studying his reflection in the mirror. "Worked here before me."

The double blinked again. Quickly, he tightened his tie, grinning. "But I never correct Mr. Ealen?" he said

Jerome nodded. He grabbed the double by his shoulders, the pressure of his hands keeping him from grabbing Jerome in the same way. "I'll be waiting." He let go, stepping out of the double's reach.

"Don't want to be late for the first time in seven years," the double said.

Before Jerome could inquire how he knew the length of his tenure, the double exited. Jerome studied himself in the mirror again, then saw the houndstooth hat on the sink. He picked it up and at seven-forty-five entered the farthest stall, where he typically found himself after his bowl of bran cereal and two cups of coffee.

As he got situated on the toilet, he was thinking five minutes. That's how long before the double would rush in, blubbering how no one believed him. Not Audrey the receptionist, who used to hide her purse beneath her desk when Jerome walked past. Nor Mr. Joseph, the chief of public relations, who also sometimes called him Gordon. From there, though, Jerome didn't know what might happen. He almost believed life would be easiest for everyone if the whole plan worked. Otherwise, Jerome supposed the man needed psychiatric help. However, he hoped the disappointment and shock of his failure might serve as a bracing blast of cold water that woke the false Jerome to reality. There was only one Jerome Manning. No need for two, besides.

At eight, Jerome flushed the toilet and exited the stall, taking care to put the hat on the counter and to keep water from splashing on his cuffs and his Timex when he washed his hands. After drying off with rough brown paper towels—a shade lighter than he—he crumpled them into a ball. The restroom door groaned as he dropped the paper into the wastebasket. Grinning, he reached for the hat but saw a heavy white man packed into a gray suit, wiping his face with a handkerchief.

Alone again in a few moments, Jerome wished for something to read. He left his newspaper, as always, in his recycling bin, and hadn't brought a paperback—Jim Thompson and Chester Himes were his favorites— because he never considered he'd be here long. He could run down the street for a *Post-Dispatch* but feared the false Jerome might arrive just after he departed and misread the real Jerome's absence as a reason to continue his faulty charade. Even if the office were empty at this hour, as Jerome guessed, or even if the public relations staff was blinded to their physical differences, something, Jerome was sure, would trip up the double. He'd be asked to make Xeroxes or attach a document on e-mail or recall some past campaign to convince the citizenry of the utility of a rate hike, one of the many tasks Jerome fulfilled each day while smiling and saying, "No problem," like a Bahamian concierge. But as more time passed and Jerome's heart surged a half-dozen times only to fall when each person entering failed to be his double, he washed his hands and buffed his shoes to a mirror-like shine.

The double returned at noon. Jerome moved forward to hug him, then grabbed him by the arms, suddenly suspicious. Why hadn't he tailed him? Because he hadn't seen the double here didn't mean he'd fooled anyone upstairs. "Where've you been?" he said.

"The office," the double said.

"Come on," Jerome said, tugging the hat on his head. It was too big, but fit him better than the double. Together, they rushed through the restroom door to the lobby. Soon they returned to the Excello, similarly empty and smoky, and sat in the same far left corner booth. The bartender with the crewcut and sore feet showed no recognition, even after they ordered two iced teas. Jerome demanded an accounting of every minute the double spent on the third floor. The double described a fairly ordinary four hours of tedium. No one acted out of character. Steve Bransby called him Jerry and Mr. Ealen asked, "How's the family, Gordon?" To the latter, the double said, "Fine! And yours?" Just as Jerome would. Then, while describing how he found Jerome's network password written on an index card underneath his desk calendar, it occurred to Jerome that he wasn't playing the joke. It was early April. His stomach felt chilled. Was someone in the office messing with him? Would he return to an office of laughing faces and have to admit how funny it was to be so easily mocked and humiliated? Yet the double's speech—incessant and giddy as a child's at an amusement park—made him doubt such an explanation. The double had been excited yesterday, but after putting his theory into practice he was convinced. He didn't echo Jerome shaking his glass of tea, trying to blunt the bitter taste. After describing how good he felt at the PR division of such an august public utility, the double paused and nodded. Jerome looked over his shoulder. The bartender stood there, no trace of detection in his hooded, weary eyes. "Anything else?" he said.

Jerome and the double shook their heads.

The bartender walked away. After a few paces he turned around, wiped a large-knuckled hand over his mouth, then said, "Are you two . . . brothers?"

Jerome and the double looked at each other, then the bartender. "No," they said at once.

Outside the Excello, Jerome donned the hat. No co-workers giggled behind stop signs or covered bus stops. "What are you going to do now?" the double said.

"I don't know," Jerome said. "I'm always at work now." Overhead, the gray sky threatened rain. Wind buffeted his cheeks as he stroked his mustache. "And no one said a word to you out of the ordinary?"

"Not even a second look," the double said. "Why don't you go to the library? Good place to spend a gray day."

"Sure," Jerome said abstractly, fighting with the wind to keep the hat on. To make it fit, he would have to let his hair grow, rather than clipping it himself every two weeks. That is, if he wanted it to fit. "But you're coming by the apartment when you get off work?" he said.

"Where else would I go?" the double said.

For the next three days, Jerome allowed the double to go to the office unattended. At noon, they met at Dusty's, a diner two streets north of the office building—Jerome was growing suspicious of the Excello's bartender—where over green salads the double regaled Jerome with an account of the morning. On Thursday Jerome stopped waking at six, Friday he stopped wearing a tie. After lunch, the double returned to the office and Jerome went to the library, where he read detective novels, then made it home to greet the double at the door of his—or was it now their?—apartment. It was only a variation on the old routine, yet Jerome didn't mind. For the first time in his adult life he was not fretting whether people measured him and his actions as representations of an entire race. He might have taken these days as an opportunity to study just who he was, had he not felt the greater need to discover why the double's ruse was working so well. The differences in height could be explained: Jerome spent most of his time at his desk. He also stooped while he walked, whether in the presence of superiors or peers. And the PR staff must have concluded that after seven mustachioed years, Jerome decided to shave. The physical dissimilarities might be evidence of his flawed perception. Perhaps he looked like the double. Hadn't he been startled the first time he heard his voice on his answering machine tape? In no way did that startled squeak correspond with the resonant tenor he felt certain emitted from his lips. Perhaps the only one who failed to see the similarities of the two Jeromes was Jerome himself.

Nonetheless, he was not ready to turn over his life. They'd still not agreed what to do with the paycheck or the lease. He didn't know if he should fear the false Jerome. At first, he seemed pitiable, a whimpering slob who believed his way up in the world was to mimic someone who hadn't had a raise in four years. Now, as the first week had come to a close, Jerome wanted to determine if audacity or psychosis motivated his double. On Saturday night, while they sat on opposite ends of the couch, each reading from his own library copy of *Cotton Comes to Harlem*, the real Jerome yawned and said, "Got a call from Granny last night." Tensely, he awaited a reply—both his grandmothers had died when Jerome was a teen—but the double didn't lower his book when he said, "Granny's been gone for years." Jerome nodded. He didn't know what else to do.

Then, on Monday, at Dusty's, the double had a question of his own.

*   *   *

"Didn't you say you'd let me take over if I convinced everybody?" the double said, forking up mashed potatoes. Jerome stared at his green salad. The double had ordered the fried chicken special, a caloric—and stereotypical—selection the real Jerome would never make. Side by side, the sat at the horseshoe-shaped counter, ten feet from the entry. Jerome sat closest to the door, in case the double tried to run. "Well?" the double said.

"You haven't convinced me," Jerome said. "You probably weigh, what, two-twenty?"

The double dabbed at a glistening line of grease on his chin. "About."

"You need to lose fifty pounds."

The double squeezed Jerome's shoulder, the first sign of physical intimacy between them and a gesture Jerome wouldn't try on a family member. "Mr. Joseph was in this morning. Said I looked like I'd been working out."

Jerome's fork clattered in his empty salad bowl. "All right," he said. "Payday's coming. We need to figure out who's going to deposit the check. You've got to keep checking in."

The double wiped his lips with the back of his hand. Jerome coughed and pointed to the napkin dispenser, as the double said, "Wouldn't have it any other way."

Jerome looked at the other patrons. In addition to its distance from the office, another reason he'd selected Dusty's was that it seemed the place where a detective might eat, and he was feeling he'd stepped into that role. As well, the clientele appeared working class—none of his peers would stop by—with a few women of color on the staff. During their previous lunches, no one had asked if they were twins or even brothers. Presently, no one glanced at him and his double. "Let's try something," Jerome said, and he waved to a black waitress. She slowly walked over, steaming coffee urn in hand. "Ain't my station," she said.

Jerome smiled broadly and touched his mustache. "I wanted to ask you something."

"Go 'head."

"Do we look alike?"

Her dull eyes turned incredulous. "You and me?"

"No, we two," he said, pointing with his thumb behind him.

"You and that man who just walked away?"

Jerome spotted the double's broad back disappearing in the shadows beneath the RESTROOMS sign. He clutched his fingers in a fist and punched the air. "Thank you," he said to the waitress. "Any time," the waitress said.

When the double returned, he picked up the check. "On me," he said.

Jerome nodded. "That's what I would have done."

"I know," the double said.

The double didn't come to the apartment that night. After hours of waiting and dozing intermittently, where he dreamed of halls of mirrors and closets filled with piles of single shoes, Jerome woke at five and haunted the lobby of the Electric Company building by six, unshaven and funky. Clad in the houndstooth hat and a trenchcoat of his own, he earned several glares from whites, though no one recognized him. By the time he realized the false Jerome might be camping out in the office, a pair of security guards was roughly escorting him outside.

Back at the apartment, he showered and dressed in a gray suit, white shirt and black tie, then arrived at Dusty's at noon. The waitress from Monday said hello and asked where his friend was. Jerome dashed to the empty Excello, startling the bartender, who said, "Iced tea, right?"

Back at his apartment, his answering machine's

message light was flashing. Jerome tripped across his spotless living room, hoping for a taunt or an excuse from the double. But the voice was that of Reverend Manning, who sounded angrier than Jerome had ever heard him: "Your mother just told me the news, boy. Seven years of hard work and you can't wake up on time? Sleeping at your desk? Didn't you remember all I told you over the years, the example I set for you and Terence?" Jerome could tell there was more, but he deleted the message. How had the double gotten their number? It didn't matter: he had to avoid this tar baby in his path.

Tossing seat cushions and stripping the unmade guest bed, Jerome looked for some significant crumb, a ticket stub or nail clipping the double had left behind. When he was stooped over the kitchen waste basket, elbow deep in coffee filters and orange peels, he realized with a cold shuddering spasm in his bowels that the double had foreseen such a search. The double had foreseen everything and took pains to leave no tracks. Jerome slumped to his immaculate kitchen floor. How long had the double known of his certain success? He'd known Jerome wouldn't confront him directly. He'd known Jerome wouldn't want to bother anyone and would realize too late his double couldn't be trusted.

He would have cried, sitting there alone on his floor, had the phone not started ringing again. Could it be? He waited for the machine to answer—he didn't want risk talking to his father—and heard his brother Terence. "Showed your color, didn't you?" he said, in a voice as carefully modulated as Jerome's—a copy of the speech their father favored. "I predicted it."

As much as Jerome wanted to answer that charge, he couldn't claim, "It's my double!" Jerome and Terence may have had only one fistfight, but each had been dueling with his brother to assure his parents that he was the one who'd taken the lessons of effacement closest to heart.

Now Terence, an assistant pharmacist at a huge discount drugstore in Denver, had no obstacle to keep him from claiming victory. Jerome lifted himself off the floor, shutting his eyes to stop envisioning the false Jerome at the DMV or in line at the new accounts window of a bank. He walked into the living room, where he picked up his copy of *Cotton Comes to Harlem*, due in a week, but let it drop, as if too weak to carry it. Instantly, he bent over to retrieve it from the carpet. While his knees groaned and his fingers reached toward the plastic covering, he realized this was an action so typical, so Jerome-like. He could almost hear his double laughing at such predictability. And that was it, he determined. No more of the old Jerome. He still had time to catch his double and re-insert himself back into the life he'd created, but he could no longer rely on routine as his guide. The way to catch the false Jerome unaware was by constructing an entirely new Jerome: unpredictable, spontaneous, more a combination of Marlowe and Shaft than the model negro he'd been so long. A feeling of certainty straightened his spine, then he remembered the book on the floor. He let it lay.

Two days later, Jerome lurked again in the alley between the shoeshine stand and the barbershop. During that forty-eight hour period, he'd slept little, ducked calls from his parents and brother, and resisted the urge to rush into the PR office. Though the April weather had warmed up, he tightened his trench coat tighter. The double had to be here soon. All criminals returned to the scene of the crime. And Jerome had traversed this stretch of sidewalk, in both directions, for over seven years. But not only did he want to catch his double, he wanted to make in his life some permanent changes. Was that why he was gave the double his chance? Because all along he'd wanted a way out of that life? Now he needed focus, hard and certain, not gauzy daydreams or cloudy visions. He shook his head.

Five minutes labored past. The streetlamps were slow in coming on, even though the sky was dark. Had the double outsmarted him? Or was he still at work? Sometimes Jerome didn't leave until seven. A soothing feeling warmed his body's core as he envisioned the false Jerome staring at one of Mr. Joseph's incomprehensible drafts. Editing speeches was never part of his job description, but Jerome had done it so many times, anymore Mr. Joseph didn't even ask him, just said, "Mark this up, Gordon." Jerome snorted, wiped his finger over his mustache, and checked his watch. Five-twenty. The trashcans hadn't been emptied, and the sweet, vegetal reek forced him to breathe through his mouth. He stood, scraping his rear against the brick wall, thinking of a bourbon at the Excello. Then the double stepped slowly past the alley, alone.

Jerome blinked, worried he might be hallucinating or fearful of what he had to do. His first time here had gone according to plan, but had he even been orchestrating the maneuvers? As he sprang, he felt secure until he gripped the double's arm. Thin as a sapling before, yet now Jerome couldn't even wrap his long fingers around the firm biceps. The double turned, yanked his arm out of Jerome's grip and crouched like a martial artist. The soft, pear-shaped body now seemed muscular and foreboding. Jerome backed away as the double's arms fell to his sides. "Oh," he said. "It's just you."

As if to prepare for a sharp, wintry wind, Jerome stiffened. "Who do you think you are?" he said. "Calling my folks."

The double laughed. "I'm a loving son who made a few mistakes," he said in Jerome's voice. Then: "Surprised they haven't fetched you home."

"Deal's off," Jerome said, leaning forward, then rocking back.

"You're not the one to decide that," the double said.

Jerome stepped forward. "You knew I'd give everything you needed?"

Beneath his still smooth upper lip, the double grinned. "You surprised me tonight. But it's still too late."

Jerome shook his head. "Give me back what's mine."

"Whose?"

Jerome advanced, but the double grabbed him by the hand, pulled him close as if in a hug between old friends. As the double walked closer to the alley, pulling him along like a doll, Jerome realized ruefully that the limp was gone.

"*Was* yours. I'm the new and improved version," the double was saying, in a voice utterly unlike Jerome's. Gravelly, deeper, more like a rapper's than an office worker's. "You're last year's model."

"Hey, Jerry," a voice shouted. The false Jerome turned, and the real one saw, over the double's shoulder, the tall, gangling figure of Steve Bransby emerging. Next to him was the shorter and stouter Mr. Ealen. Both were waving, which thrilled Jerome, though he'd never in his life been excited to see either. Still, a new opportunity stood before him, and it resulted from taking a risk, the first significant action of this newest Jerome. The two white men would see the dissimilarities now, as he stood next to the double, under the streetlamp's beam, as if in a lineup—a forum, he sensed, that whites used to distinguish one black from another for centuries. But surely Bransby and Ealen would realize they'd been duped by this imposter. Jerome's bizarre odyssey would finally end. The double would be arrested, and it probably wouldn't be the first time. Jerome struggled to face his fellow PR men, but the double pushed him toward the shadows of the alley. They faced each other, and the real Jerome grinned. Opposite stood a man who looked nothing like him. Everything could now return to normal. Once he thought that, he amended himself: things wouldn't return to normal. He didn't know what changes he might make, only that there would be some soon. "Jerry," Steve Bransby called again, as he and Mr. Ealen neared. "Headed home?" Mr. Ealen said, tapping cigarette ash on the sidewalk.

Jerome tried to speak, but the double stepped suddenly on his foot. "That's right," the false Jerome said. "And you, sir?"

"Thought I might have a pop first."

"Interested, Jerry?" Steve said. He looked toward Jerome, then blinked and turned to the double.

Dragging one foot over his sore one, Jerome stepped closer to the light from the streetlamp. Neither Bransby nor Ealen looked at him. Never before had he been asked for a post-work drink. Or had he? His father's edicts would have kept him away, for Rev. Manning preached it didn't matter if a black man consumed a thimbleful around whites. In their minds it was a quart. "Sure thing," the double said, in a voice so like Jerome's that the three were walking down the street before Jerome could get over the shock. Bransby turned around and Jerome started after him but stopped when he heard the man say, "Who's that, Jerry?"

"Someone I used to know," the double said.

A week later, Jerome was walking up the steps of the library, book in hand. He wanted the transaction to be simple, so he was there at closing time, prepared to drop the book in the after-hours slot. Though nothing of the sort had happened at the dry-cleaner or the bank or the grocery, Jerome still approached every interaction fearfully, certain he'd be informed of bills that needed paying immediately or insufficient funds in his accounts, some sign that the double was enjoying his life with Jerome's earnings, present and past. He checked his Timex. Early by a few minutes—a symptom of the old Jerome, a self he feared he might never lose.

The lights dimmed inside the library and he saw employees gathering. He envied them and missed the regularity of his former days. But with no job and no purpose—the double had won, of that he was certain—what was the point of setting his alarm? He'd spent most of his time trying to summon the nerve to speak to his father, who was leaving messages every day and threatening to smack some sense into his youngest.

As the slow-moving second hand of his Timex swept away another minute, Jerome reached for the library's front door. He gripped the handle and pulled it open, hearing the harsh notes of male laughter close behind. Nowadays laughter seemed always nearby. He let go the handle as a group of black men in pea-green uniforms and work boots mounted the steps. They were laughing but not at him. They didn't look his way as they entered the vestibule, save for one, a broad shouldered, brown-skinned fellow with a jheri curl. He said, "Nice brim."

Blinking, Jerome stared, his hands rising toward the houndstooth hat he now wore whenever he was out. As he hadn't cut his hair in three weeks, the hat fit much better. He nodded at the man, who stood on the top step. "Waiting for someone?" the man said.

Jerome shook his head, said nothing. He hadn't spoken to anyone all day and his voice seemed to have migrated to a foreign part of his body.

"Thought you might be the new man," the fellow said. "Oh well, back to the slave." He pulled open the door. As the library workers and few remaining patrons streamed out, Jerome found his voice. "New man?" he said.

"On the cleaning crew," the man said. "Been needing another janitor for two months."

"Oh," Jerome said.

"You looking for work? Hold on." He entered the library and Jerome dropped the book in the after hours slot. The man returned and handed to Jerome a job description, application. "Call that number," the man said, pointing to it with a gloved finger. "Could use us another man." He paused. "Especially another brother."

Jerome looked at the man's smiling round face, then the nametag stitched above his right breast pocket. "Thanks, Will," Jerome said.

The man blinked, then laughed. He touched the oval nametag and said, "Got this from the dude used to work here before me. They call me Cap." He angled his gloved hand toward Jerome. After a second Jerome, offered his own, surprised by Cap's sudden soul grip, a handshake he hadn't used in years.

Back at his building, Jerome slowly walked up two flights, reading the application. He'd never worked custodial before. He'd gone to college, Terence too, because Mr. and Mrs. Manning wanted their sons to rise above such menial labor. Yet there were good benefits, and it was union. Still, he was nowhere near thinking of applying when he neared his apartment door and saw the clasped manila envelope tilted against it. He wanted to rush down out to the sidewalk—only one person would leave the folder—yet he checked the impulse. His past experience with the false Jerome showed he should leave him alone.

Inside his apartment, he opened the envelope and shook out a laminated social security card, a bankbook and a note. It was typed and unsigned, but Jerome recognized the paper from the pile of twenty-weight bond on his former desk. It read, "Go to the DMV. Make sure you get a white clerk. Then report your driver's license missing and get a new photo. And don't worry about your money. Just look in the bankbook. Money I already had. I wanted your life."

Jerome stepped heavily but directly to his living room window and opened it. He stood still and listened. No laughter echoed from the streets. The message light blinked on his answering machine. He ignored it. Without looking at the bankbook, he sensed every dime he'd earned was in a new account, under the name on the social security card, Roger Henderson. Had the double been Roger? Or had he swapped roles with another? He didn't need to know. Instead, he said the name aloud and repeated it for a few minutes so he could remember the next day when he called the number for that custodial job.

Once his soft hands fitted themselves to the handles of mops and pushbrooms, once his nose stopped shrinking at the odiferous restrooms and the chemicals used to clean them, Jerome became a valued member of the custodial crew. Evenings were, he discovered, the perfect time to work. He shut his blackout windows and fell asleep by nine or ten in the morning, then woke at six, read his newspaper over a leisurely breakfast. With a week's worth of uniforms in his closet, he didn't fret over what combinations might dress him suitably. Initially, he was always first on the library's steps, then he timed his arrival to coincide with that of the other crew members. Later, he arrived with the rest with no effort at all. At work, he no longer felt measuring eyes. He spoke often and loudly, even when he didn't know much or was completely wrong about the subject, whether it was politics, religion or sports.

On weekends, he met Cap and the others, Wilson,

J.C., and Ed, and lounged around barbershops, where he let professional manage his hair and mustache, or dined at rib joints and fried fish places in parts of town he'd never explored. He viewed NBA and NFL games on Cap's wide screen and went on double dates with attractive women he never would have met, to clubs he never would have heard of had he spent the rest of his days in public relations. Rare was the Saturday or Sunday evening when he was not out somewhere, rarer still was he ever alone in his apartment, snacking while he read of or viewed detectives in action.

Rev. Manning's flat statement that he had no use with a janitor for a son removed any worries about a family visit and the confusion it might breed. Terence could claim victory and celebrate in his one bedroom apartment in suburban Denver. Jerome forgave him for every hurtful word he'd said, because he didn't care about Jerome. He claimed to be what his I.D. cards asserted: Roger Henderson. He only wished he could tell everyone who'd known him before, including the new Jerome, who needed to hear how thankful he was to be Roger, though he suspected they'd never meet again.

Yet many months later, he spotted his double. The two were headed in separate directions, on the other side of the street, but almost directly across the alley between the barbershop and shoeshine stand where the first of their face-to-face encounters occurred. Roger, on his way to a union meeting, recognized the striped tie first, and touched his work-worn fingers to his pea-green shirt, noting the double had mastered a single-windsor. He might have paused and slipped past the other pedestrians, then suggested they stop by the Excello to catch up, but his meeting was in ten minutes and the double also appeared rushed. Instead, Roger nodded, as did the double, in the manner of black men surrounded by those unlike them. Some grit in the air made Roger blink, but as they passed, never to see one another again, he could have sworn the look on the double's face was one of regret.

Among the Wild Mulattos

Not long ago, at the beginning of this new century, I received from my maternal uncle a rather fateful phone call. I hadn't spoken to Uncle Dalton in years, hadn't seen him since my high school graduation, when he whispered that if I moved far enough away from my parents' northeastern home, with my complexion, manner and intellect, I might pass for white. His calling surprised me, as did the frantic tone with which he relayed a curious adventure. He and some friends had been drinking and duck hunting in the Arkansas Delta, and through some sequence of events he could not fully explain, he got lost among the oxbow lakes, sloughs and uninhabited woods along the Mississippi River. For two days he wandered, convinced he'd die, with no map and his ammunition depleted from shooting at canvasbacks and trying to signal his companions. But on the third day, when he was making peace with God—in large part requesting forgiveness for the execrable treatment he'd given my mother for marrying my father—while falling to his knees he saw a slim youth in what looked like a gray sweatsuit, stepping into a gap among trees and thigh-high weeds. Stumbling forward, my uncle called for help, and the boy emerged, told my uncle to break his rifle, toss it to the ground and wait right there. In a few minutes the youth returned with venison jerky, a rough ceramic jug of fresh water, and a hand drawn map on homemade paper that steered Uncle Dalton to a gas station several circuitous miles down a dirt road. "And he looked just like you," my uncle insisted. "Just like you."

I thanked Uncle Dalton for the call, wished him well, but made no plans to verify his claims. Much could explain his story, such as the fact he'd been in a bourbon-induced stupor and dreamed the whole thing. The only other mulatto he had ever seen was me and rarely at that. Long before his call, though, I'd heard of hidden societies of mulattos. In Ancient Civilizations, an undergraduate survey, my instructor lectured for a week on great hoaxes, primarily to show how easy it was to manipulate people into believing anything about our ancestors. Included among these lectures was the Cardiff Giant, Piltdown Man, the Tasadays of the Philippines, and, as my instructor called it, "the fabled island of the Mulattos." During this lecture, I did not raise my hand, as it was a large class, and in those days, I rarely did anything that pointed me out as a mulatto.

Yet I wanted to know then what made my professor so certain it was a hoax, and why he dismissed what he called "the fever dream of lonely explorers." The notion of a group of mulattos living in some idyllic haven for generations, out of the reach of society's arms, did not strike me as unlikely. My father, the single black executive of an insurance company, had been transferred half a dozen times when I was growing up, and wherever we landed I was the only biracial child and required to explain to my new peers how such anomalies as my parents occurred. An all-mulatto society sounded like an opportunity I would have sacrificed much to join. After my undergraduate education, though, when I'd been seduced by the daring and intrigue that came with being an anthropology professor, I discovered the book claiming the existence of the island—a self-published travel journal called, *A Year Among the Wild Mulattos of the Caribbean*, by a German named Hans Zimmer—and begrudgingly admitted my professor was likely right. Still, I never entirely forgot the wild mulattos and encountered every few years in my reading a new fanciful notion of such a people. In one article they were considered a Lost Tribe of Israel, in another coevals with the mysterious Moundbuilders. True believers postulated them as escapees from Atlantis, while a radical sect of Mormons asserted the mulattos of legend encountered Christ during his sojourn to the New World. Each claim appeared easier to dismiss than the last, and sense told me the only place a colony of mulattos existed was in the daydreams of the lonesome biracial child I'd been. As I traveled, publishing articles about living among African pygmies, Australian bushmen, and Detroit Crips, I encountered few other mulattos, and heard not even a rumor of a wild band's existence.

Months after his call, though, I could not forget my uncle's tale of a lone mulatto appearing at the mouth of a wooded area. We mulattos always seemed a more cosmopolitan people, at home in cities until the pressure of being neither white nor black and yet both caused us to succumb to our various crises of identity. Still, the image my uncle provided kept sliding closer and closer to the hope I held out for the wild mulattos' reality. The two thoughts crashed together when I began a sabbatical for a semester—ostensibly to write about some recent travels in the former Soviet Union—and I determined I needed to at least investigate my uncle's claim. Prepared to spend no more than a few days exploring, I expected little but confirmation that the nay-sayers had been right all along. After a Greyhound Bus to Helena, Arkansas, I backpacked south, staying near the Mississippi's many bends and bows, trying to find a spot like that my uncle had described. Naturally, he'd lost the map that brought him to safety, and I was fairly sure, after a good forty hours, that the main cause of his vision was his two days' deprivation and the certainty he was going to die. During that time, I swatted giant mosquitoes immune to repellent and ate nearly all my trail mix and dried figs. I was ready to turn back and blot out for good this notion. A hidden society of mulattos, my sensible self said. What kind of lunatic would even believe? But that's when a group of children playing in a clearing appeared, barefoot and bare-chested, their fawn skins slick with sweat, their green eyes glowing in the dusk like emeralds.

As far as I could gather from them, this particular group of mulattos had never been in the Caribbean, where Hans Zimmer placed his mythical band. Nor did any of the members claim a lineage to such a region. They were not at all savage. None, in Zimmer's heated English (his third language after German and Polish), would "likely slice you ear to ear as ask for the time of day." At first, they were more frightened of me than I of them. They feared the influences I might bring, as an outsider, especially to the children, who, I learned, were free to leave once they turned sixteen. They might also join those who worked in the outer world, which everyone called Two Box, as in the two boxes one had to choose from on applications and the like: "White" or "Black." Yet even with this freedom, only one or two departed every few years, and of those, most eventually returned.

For an hour or two, at first, I was kept outside of what they simply called "the Compound." The children who brought me by the hand to one of the entrances were spirited away, soon replaced by five elders who decided after some debate to let me enter provided that I, unlike Socrates, promised not to corrupt the youth. I could stay as long as I wanted, I was told, though they blindfolded me and made me surrender my camera and the entire contents of my backpack, save for my wallet, which was secured in a secret inner pocket. When the leader, one Mr. Gerald, asked what I did for a living, I lied, figuring an anthropologist would not gain entry to this fascinating world. So I told him the profession I'd given myself to answer people in airports and in taxis: a waterbed salesman. No one ever asked another question after that in the outside world, and it made the mulattos blink and remain quiet, as if trying to figure out why anybody would earn his living that way.

Once among the entire group—my best estimate is that there were ninety—it was clear all knew I was one of them. In my world, I'd always been a bit of an anomaly: not only biracial but light-skinned and blue-eyed, so many—black and white—never thought to think I might not be white. In my earliest observation, though, I noticed skin color—such currency among Americans of African descent—mattered not at all among these mulattos, even though there was no uniformity of color among them, their shades ranging from the lightest of light to just darker than café au lait. But as the living situation was communal, none asserted any light- or dark-skinned privilege or primacy among his peers.

The land itself had once been the property of a hunting club, which accounted for the large wooden lodge in the center of the compound, holding the kitchen, dining area, laundry facilities, restrooms and schoolrooms that the over thirty families used. Before that, according to Mr. Gerald, the oldest of the elders, they'd lived in Louisiana swamp country, but emigrated during Huey Long's senatorship, when one of their number defected, threatening to expose them to Two Box. They feared there'd soon be no place where mulattos could avoid the limiting expectations placed upon them by both whites and blacks. That had been the original impetus of the first exodus, that which sent the progenitors Geraldine and Roscoe Pretty and three other families—the Brights, Darlings and Butlers—to the wilds at the end of the nineteenth century: In Two Box, as they saw it, a mulatto was forced to choose. You had to be one or the other. After you chose, everyone complained you weren't black or white enough. Or weren't sharing your color with your darker brethren. Or weren't talking the right kind of English. When I first heard this, I felt a pang of sympathy, then wanted to claim things were different now. On the census there was an "Other" category. People of multiple backgrounds could check as many boxes as they wished (though I only ever checked African American). But at the time I was in the presence of the children I first saw, Stephanie, Lee-Lee and Monroe—he'd been the one who met my uncle—and based on my promise, kept quiet. When I finally told Mr. Darnell, my earliest guide, he laughed, showing a perfect set of white teeth, then said, "You call that progress?"

Mr. Darnell was a Natural, meaning he traced his lineage all the way back to the Prettys or the other families. They made up perhaps eighty percent of the group, while the rest, called Assimilateds, came from all over but landed at some time in Memphis, where they ultimately desired to drop out of their Two Box lives and through chance meetings with the Naturals, joined the Compound. Mr. Darnell was also a Wage-Earner, which meant he rose early every weekday morning, performed his toilet in the men's washroom at the lodge, then rode in a van with the others to Memphis, where they worked, typically in solitary pursuits—custodians, parking attendants, security guards; they called themselves Wage Earners to remind themselves why they were in Two Box: to earn a wage.

Along with the monies brought in by the Wage Earners, the mulattos could depend upon more from their rental properties, and four times a month the Collectors—four women, one of whom was Mrs. Earlene, Mr. Darnell's wife—rode in the van with the Wage Earners. All this astonished me, expecting, as I did, a rustic group in torn clothes, spearing fish with sharpened sticks, slumbering beneath the stars; but I came to understand Wage Earners and Collectors traveled to Two Box with a heavy burden. "Nothing looks better," Mrs. Earlene once said, "than Memphis in the rear view mirror." They were trying to accumulate enough properties in order to end the working days of the Wage Earners, inverting the priority of the two enterprises, as the first apartment building had been bought by Mr. Pretty—passing for white—so the Earners could have a street address to give employers. It's worth pointing out here that had these mulattos not chosen to distance themselves from my world, they would have been considered upright citizens by most. Though they never voted—who ever represented them?—nor sent their children to public school—who would teach them what they needed to know?—they did pay all manner of taxes on time and ran splendid, clean apartments that all had tenant waiting lists. They didn't want a majority of their lives to transpire in Two Box, and as my stay lengthened, I understood why this was so.

I had no plans for how long I'd stay, at first. A week passed and I wasn't even sure it was seven days. My best measurement of time was the beard and long hair I'd grown, but a barber named Mr. Chester gave me the finest haircut and shave I'd ever had, treating my scalp and skin as if they were his own. Meals were prepared by the kitchen staff four times a day, the cuisine heavy on vegetables and grains, but with some game, poultry and fish. I left my clothes each day in a basket outside the single-room cabin assigned me (a widow, Mrs. Belle, had died at ninety-seven, leaving the vacancy) and found them there folded neatly the next morning. No one asked me to hunt or fish or plow. No one asked me to do much of anything.

Most of the time I spent observing. I learned all believed in a merciful god, though without any of the interor intrafaith schisms that existed outside the Compound. Gender-specific tasks could not be seen, as some males cooked and washed clothes, while some females led hunting expeditions. Age did not automatically produce authority, nor was it seen as infirmity: Elders toiled as hard as adults, especially when they pored over *Business Week* and *Wall Street Journal* to determine stock purchases and mutual fund transfers. At school, the children learned how to raise livestock, sew, hunt, reason, write and read (a popular book was Nella Larsen's *Passing*, selected, the adults privately admitted, as anti-Two Box propaganda). Yet whenever I drifted too close to the classrooms, an adult would engage me in conversation. Never about the outside world and typically guiding me toward questions about whether I found their living situation as ideal as they. Though I knew about Naturals and Assimilateds by this time, I did not suspect anyone was trying to recruit me into staying. I thought they were trying to keep the children free of my taint. None should have feared. The children were not eager to learn of TV shows and fashion and fast food. They were as happy as their parents in the paradisiacal surroundings, having never spent an hour in the world that had shaped me.

Soon, though, one person in particular was standing between me and the children, even though she was little more than a child herself. Teena was her name (only after marrying did one receive a title), and she was nineteen, three years past the age at which she could have left. That decision, she claimed, was so easy to make she didn't even announce if she was staying or going. On her sixteenth birthday, she woke up, washed, and went to the pens to feed the chickens and search for eggs. For some sixteen-year-olds, a ceremony called The Choosing was held. Teena said this was received by parents and elders as a worrisome sign: those who went through the ceremony occasionally departed, including her own cousin, who ten years earlier had chosen to live among the meddlesome citizens of the United States. No news had been learned from or of him since.

It did not take long to recognize that as well as being an easy person to talk with, Teena was a beautiful, young woman. A shade under six feet tall, she had brown hair with blond streaks cropped bluntly at chin level, eyes as green as new money and a lithe, athletic figure. Beneath the leafy canopy of the Compound, Teena was gracious, selfless and, I discovered when I tripped over a tree root and she kept me from falling, strong. In my world, modeling agencies and basketball coaches would have warred for her services. Nineteen years my junior, she spoke with the intelligence of an adult, and the body beneath her overalls and flannel shirts was certainly mature. Still, that she squealed with delight at every spotted fawn or hopping frog suggested to me an innocence that could not be found among young women her age beyond these wooded boundaries.

Soon I was meeting Teena once a day after lunch. Planning on it, as well. Sitting at whichever family table I was invited to that day, I fed myself and stared, nearly oblivious to all near me, waiting for the moment she left Mrs. Earlene and her younger siblings, of whom Lee-Lee was one, so that I might time my departure from the lodge to coincide with hers. Though I'd just broken up with a woman—the second I nearly married—I resorted to these junior high maneuvers, hoping I might, with caution and courtesy, gain some approval from the elders. Little review of my actions reached me during my second and third weeks, but in the middle of my fourth, I thought I discovered Teena had designs of her own.

I'd been invited to hunt with some of the skilled men and women, led by a pair of fifteen-year-old giants named Enos and Joel, but I shied away, almost claiming my hand was shaped more for a camera, then stammered about being a city boy. Foolishly, I held up my soft hands as if these were primitives with whom I needed sign language to communicate. Among the Assimilateds were college graduates, one, Mr. Clyde, with a Wharton School MBA, who advised Memphians of all ethnicities about their finances and who also made sure the Compound's assets matured handsomely. The hunters laughed and questioned whether all those waterbeds I sold had left me forgetful of my natural instincts. Shortly after they pushed into the woods, Teena arrived—as if on cue, it later seemed—and asked if I wanted to stroll in a different direction. I agreed.

Autumn had definitely arrived: the leaves now coppery as some of the darker mulattos, the air clean and scented with earth and river water, but the chill of morning lingered longer and longer into the afternoon. I could smell woodsmoke that day, as well as the scent of homemade soap exuding from Teena, who stood near enough to kiss. She lead me through a small opening behind the lodge, near where the vans were kept and the keys hung from hooks bolted to the rear wall. Soon the path narrowed and we were pushing branches out of the way while leaves obscured the thin, yellow sun. For some time, we didn't speak, but when we arrived at a small clearing, Teena started talking about how happy she was that I'd come to the Compound. Perhaps for five minutes she relayed a number of reasons why I made her so happy. We had so much in common, she gushed. I was only a little bit taller than she. I made her feel so much smarter than her parents and siblings did. I listened, smiling, but could not see why she'd dragged me through the forest to share this information. I interrupted her: "Why did you need to say all this now? And why here?"

"Because I love you," she said. Then her body became a sudden and lunging force that pinned me against a tree trunk. Her mouth covered mine sloppily. With the force of a Dale Carnegie student's handshake, she grabbed my crotch. Open-eyed and baffled, I pushed her away, but Teena strained forward, murmuring, "I loved you since the first day the elders allowed you to stay." So much traveled through my mind then: her age, my intentions here, the fact that I did have a life back home, utility bills, a mortgage, a pint of rocky road ice cream in the freezer. Never did I think—my triceps trembling from fending her off—that this clumsy seduction was anything but Teena's idea. Eyes closed, mouth opened as wide as is suggested for performing CPR, she looked so young, though at the same time the most beautiful woman I'd seen. All my adult life, I'd been looking for her, it occurred to me. I'd dated a Lebanese woman, African-, Korean- and Japanese-Americans, Anglos. I'd been engaged for the past year to a Czech med student named Marta, but never had I a friendship with another mulatto, especially one so wonderful as Teena. When I relaxed and met her lips with mine, though, I reveled at the pressure of her hands on my arms and clutched at her body as if it might disappear. Then I halted. I suffered no bout of guilt or saw the nineteen years difference between us as starkly as her wide, unlined forehead, the color of cream-heavy tea. No, I didn't want to proceed until I knew I had protection. "Wait," I said, and reached in my jeans for my wallet—a ridiculous encumbrance I'd yet to shed—but as my fingers touched the leather I knew no condom was inside. I put it back into my pocket and said, "I don't have a rubber."

This statement fetched a look of confusion, the first I'd seen on Teena's face. "Rubbers," she said. "For what? This?" Then she mimed holding an umbrella and jumping and splashing into imaginary rain puddles. And though my desire for her still flickered deep within me— and never really abated—I hugged her close, smelled her clean hair and kissed the crown of her head. "You're too good to be true," I said. Later, I would learn how apt this statement was, but for now I didn't know, and wouldn't have cared if I did.

Looking back, my worldly concerns were a blessing, though Teena's attempted seduction still created significant change in my life. The next Monday, I commuted to Memphis with the Wage Earners (blindfolded until we were on Highway 61) and spent much of the morning and afternoon on the phone. I found a pair of students to house-sit and tend my lawn and garden. I canceled magazine subscriptions, moved money around (thanks to a tip from Mr. Clyde) and on the blindfolded ride back to the Compound, I felt I'd done all I could to assure my stay was open ended. No potential reasons for an exit occurred to me, especially when I was allowed to remove the blindfold and saw Teena waiting near the lodge. At the time, I thought it ironic that once I feared I might corrupt her, yet here we were, some two days from her aborted attempt at corrupting me. That night, I sat at her table, but while we ate grilled chicken, greens and baked sweet potatoes and drank homemade muscadine wine I did not notice the proprietary eyes of Mrs. Earlene and Mr. Darnell.

But in the days that followed, because I'd made it so clear to all I was staying indefinitely, the simple days of observation and pleasant walks ended. No longer a guest, I was asked to do my share of the labor. Knowing me as they did, though, they expected very little. That's how it appeared as the elders assigned me duties in the kitchen one day, checking trotlines and seines at the river the next, then sending me out to prepare the fields for fall planting. Whoever supervised shook his head at all my endeavors, which, I must admit, did not come to me naturally. I still worked hard and most nights, even if I could have spent some time alone with Teena, I was too fatigued to show her the use of the Nonoxynol-9 Trojans I'd bought at a Rite Aid in downtown Memphis. But after that Monday I was not seated at her table. Nor did we spend any time together afterward. She smiled whenever we passed, and once she knitted her hands over her heart and mouthed "I love you"—the gesture nearly felled me—but for over a week I didn't get near enough to touch her or inhale her sweet, humble scent.

Meanwhile, the time had come for Enos and Joel to make their decisions. Born on the same day to different mothers, the two giants had lived like brothers, and both had requested—to the dismay of the elders—the ceremony of The Choosing. Scheduled for nightfall, just after dinner had been eaten and all the washing done—on kitchen duty, I broke two glasses—it was a ceremony I was excited to witness, though disappointed I had no camera with which to document it. Still, I had pocketed a pen from the Bank of America office and from the schoolroom in the lodge I'd swiped plenty of the homemade paper my uncle had claimed to receive.

In the middle of the Compound, a bonfire raged, and all the elders stood around it in a circle. The rest of us stood off to one side, solemnly chanting "Come." I looked for but could not find Teena, so I concentrated on the Choosing. The chanting stopped when Enos and Joel appeared, flanked by their parents, the four men nearly seven feet tall and the mothers easily six-two. Stripped to the waist, Enos and Joel wore what looked like the breechclout Hollywood straps on all its Indians. The evening's chill numbed my fingers but the boys kept their jaws tight and would not tremble as they halted before the circle of elders. The boys embraced their mothers, who joined the crowd. Two elders stepped aside, and Mr. Gerald walked forward, dressed in what looked like a buckskin jacket. Though his lineage in most instances would have made him a ruler, he went out of his way to keep himself among the people, working not as a Wage Earner but toiling among the launderers. Flanked by other elders, Mr. Gerald held up two suitcases, then set them down. Next, he held up two bus tickets, followed by two suits with white shirts, ties, and hard soled shoes. All these items he laid solemnly on the suitcases, then intoned, through his steamy breath, "Come, Enos and Joel, to make your Choosing." Firelight flickered over both boys' faces. Each ran his fingers over the clothes. Joel even tried on the shoes and walked around the bonfire. After the ceremony, I learned the two had appeared restless in the year between this birthday and the one previous. And I certainly saw, in the moments preceding their eventual decisions, a number of Naturals and Assimilateds suddenly looking away, as if unable to bear the wait. Eventually, though, after Joel shed the shoes, each boy stepped back outside the ring of elders. Mr. Gerald stepped forward and gestured to the suitcases, piled with goodies. "You have chosen?" he said.

Gravely, both boys nodded.

"Then," Mr. Gerald said, "The Choosing is done."

Bottles of muscadine wine and cornsilk liquor appeared, and every adult in the Compound celebrated Enos and Joel's decision to stay. The temperature I judged to be in the thirties, but only Mr. Gerald and I wore a coat among the males, as the others had joined Enos and Joel in stripping off their shirts. Vainly, I scanned the crowd for Teena but softened that disappointment with the thought to go to my cabin and write some notes. But as I trotted that way, Mr. Gerald—I could see now he wore a tan Members Only jacket—stood in my path and placed one hand on the small of my back. "Did you enjoy the ceremony?" he said, placing firm pressure on me. At my height, he was one of the smaller Naturals, but his strength was evident. Soon he was pushing me toward a seat on a felled log.

I nodded and said, "Fascinating," which is how I felt, though I wanted still to write down my impressions and observations, lest I forget any detail. I stopped resisting, though—this was Mr. Gerald—and sat down with him on the log.

"As an outsider, you might not know this," he said, "but we were worried about those two."

"Really?"

"Drink?' Mr. Gerald offered a flat pint of clear liquor to me. Among the many local beverages I'd consumed in my travels, the worst was a concoction of fermented human saliva and ground red ants served by an indigenous tribe in the Amazon basin. A little moonshine wasn't going to hurt, though its unregulated potency shot flames to my head. The bonfire popped and crackled as Mr. Gerald took back the bottle, sipped from it, then said, "Every time we have a Choosing, especially with young men, I worry."

"Why?"

"Because they're most likely to leave. Because of them, we weren't going to let you join us. Your wordliness might have been the push off the cliff."

"I'm glad it didn't happen."

"Oh no, you've behaved just as we asked." As he passed me the bottle, I kept my eyes open but had no luck in finding Teena. All the women seemed to have vanished. Mr. Gerald said, "I hear you've been trying your best to do your part around here."

I sputtered some liquor on the ground, my head a little seasick, then turned to nod.

"Even if there haven't been the best results, your effort is appreciated." He paused, corked the bottle when I handed it back to him. "How do you think, though, you might best be able to help us?"

Without pausing to consider his motives—or why he suddenly was speaking to me at all—I almost mentioned I should be in the schoolroom. Two more swallows and I'd be babbling, yet even in the impending drunk I knew I shouldn't tread in that direction. What would a waterbed salesman be able to teach their bright and gifted offspring? I shook my head. "I don't know, sir."

Mr. Gerald stood from the log. "You'll figure it out," he said, fitting the bottle in one pocket, while retrieving something else from the other. "This might help." He handed to me a tightly folded wand of newspaper, which turned out to be the Want Ads from the *Commercial Appeal*. And, as I'd learn moments later in my cabin, Mr. Gerald had gone to the trouble of underlining in pencil a number of open positions in Sales.

The next morning, I traveled again with the Wage-Earners, blindfolded much of the way, wearing one of the suits that had been set out for Enos and Joel in the Choosing. As if fit me well, I wondered if the elders intended to outfit these two so poorly that they'd be laughed back to the Compound. Nonetheless, I was intent on trying to gain a sales job. I'd received from my fellow mulattos so much but had given in return practically nothing. I also hoped a job might aid me in my pursuit of Teena, whose nude form I conjured up every night in my cabin.

In Memphis, after Mr. Clyde pulled the van into the parking lot of his office, I was on my own. Driving felt strange at first: my hands could not grip the steering wheel, and my feet felt too heavy for the accelerator and the brake pedal. Traffic I would have been inured to back home seemed dangerous as I drove to the first stop on my list, a furniture store in Midtown. But I struck out there and all others subsequent that day, as everyone who interviewed me appeared to know instantly I'd never sold a thing other than old furniture at yard sales. I hated disappointing the mulattos on the Compound with my sorry news, yet I was also trying to figure out a way to tell them that though the man they knew was not the man I truly was, they had nothing to fear. Yes, I was observing them as I had with other tribes and bands of people across the globe, but I would gladly put all those tasks aside, cancel any thoughts of recording for posterity their ways and customs. For I believed then if I could marry Teena, the only time I'd leave would be to secure my money, sell my house and belongings to aid the removal from Two Box.

The next morning, I discovered an open position at an outdoor sports equipment store, where my knowledge and the manager's laid-back attitude put me in the lucky position of having a job and securing a more definitive position at the Compound. A Wage Earner who was moving toward being an Assimilated, was how I characterized myself then, wondering if there'd be a ceremony to accompany my choice. And after a week of work, I was invited regularly to Mr. Darnell and Mrs. Earlene's table, across from the sunny Lee-Lee, my knee warm against Teena's. After I handed over my first two weeks' pay, that next Friday, Teena knocked at my cabin door on Saturday morning, and we spent the rest of the day together, holding hands, strolling the Compound, viewed by all the others. Every single one had for us a smile.

But for all this positive development, my visits to

Memphis five days a week—including some Saturdays and Sundays—troubled me. Before, in the idyllic company of all the mulattos, I could only envision my world as they saw it. They were, after all, most correct. A mulatto in Two Box was subject to the worst kind of stupidity and intolerance and from all sides. For every Anglo like my uncle who pretended I didn't exist so he wouldn't have to admit his niece had had intercourse with a black man, there was a black man who sneered when I tried to find solidarity with him. Avoiding that nonsense seemed the Compound's greatest virtue. However, even though in my first two weeks at the Rugged Edge, I'd been asked about my ethnicity by several customers and three co-workers, I was detecting what the mulattos definitely didn't want their sixteen-year-olds to know of: the wonderful variety of post-modern America.

I'd been away only a couple of months, yet much change had occurred. A new Halle Berry movie was out. Lenny Kravitz appeared on commercials for the Gap. Coke now had a lemon-flavored model. Ads for a steak burrito at Taco Bell suddenly resounded with the promise of eternal life. Nightly, I'd forget this stimuli when I jotted down my notes of life among the mulattos or when Teena would visit. But every morning, behind my blindfold, I was envisioning what I might see, and every night, blindfolded again, I reviewed all the temptations dangled before me anew until soon I couldn't wait for every trip with the Wage Earners to begin.

Things worsened when I saw Enos and Joel one Sunday afternoon. Standing side by side behind the lodge, close to where the vans were parked, each would leap and smack his hand against the building, trying to outdo the other. Consistently, their hands touched a spot I marked at eleven-and-a-half or twelve feet and this in their bare feet on hard-packed earth on a day no warmer than thirty-two. Had I not been going to Memphis so much, I might have said what I eventually did, but in the break room at work the Grizzlies' season was a common topic, and I could recite their starting five and knew they had a three-game swing in California starting that night. Joel smacked the wall so hard the van keys fell from their hook, and I said, "You two would be superstars in hoops." After the looks of befuddlement, they wanted me to explain. I replaced the keys and treated the boys to a brief account of the game but left them looking still bewildered, massive hands on their powerful hips.

A few nights later, while I was walking past the laundry to steal more homemade paper, Mr. Gerald appeared and asked me how work was going. I told him well, but then he strode closer and whispered that I needed to be sure I left all that was Memphis in Memphis. Apparently, the boys had fashioned a crude rim and were keeping everyone in their family's cabins awake with their nocturnal jostling. The next night Teena did not greet me at the lodge when I returned from a day's work. I was being punished, and everyone knew what hurt me most.

So I promised myself to honor Mr. Gerald's request, but while in Memphis my attentions kept drifting. I dined at Indian and Vietnamese restaurants, drank cup after cup of coffee, and even smoked a few Marlboros though I don't know how to properly inhale. Some days I pretended I had a shift when in fact I browsed bookstores and watched movies, drank draft beers in dark bars and impressed patrons with my answers to *Jeopardy* questions. Once, for the first time in my life, I sat in a mall and just watched the customers, the vast array of classes and colors and sizes and shapes so dazzling, I wondered why I'd not written an article on this phenomenon before. At the Compound, I behaved as I was supposed to. When the boys urged me to tell them more about basketball, I shrugged and walked away in full view of Mr. Gerald and his wife, Mrs. Nadine. In a few days, I had again the company of Teena. More than once, we heard from her parents and others that we looked so good together, and I heard whispers about upcoming wedding ceremonies. At night, though, I'd be seized in my cabin by the sense a decision had to be made. I couldn't live two lives—one worldly, the other humble—and expect to keep them entirely separate. Rather than settling that dilemma, I found ways to forget it, typically in the form of Teena.

But when she and I finally consummated our relationship, the damage I feared was fully visited on me. After demonstrating to her the use of three Trojans on successive nights, I felt as though I now had a complete satisfaction. All the petty pursuits in Memphis could be put aside. I had what I had long cherished. From observation and discussion with other members of the Compound, I'd gleaned that there was no prohibition against premarital sex, but an understanding existed that the two parties would almost always eventually marry. And I was more than willing now to commit myself. I could envision a life with Teena. A true and blessed one. I even imagined what our children would look like when I used up all the Trojans. I was in the place most like home I'd ever been. Why leave?

But while I dreamed and readied myself for a lifetime, Teena was apparently talking to Lee-Lee, who told their mother, and after a return trip from Memphis, I took off my blindfold and saw most of the elders standing by the lodge. Teena stood with them, both arms gripped by her mother, and eventually her father when he caught wind of why everyone was gathered. Mr. Gerald stepped toward me. He said, "I asked you to keep that which was Memphis in Memphis."

I said nothing, thinking of all my misbehaviors, the most recent of which was gorging on sashimi and drinking Asahi at a downtown sushi bar, but nothing, I believed, had followed me back to the Compound. I couldn't think of what I'd done here that might be wrong until Mr. Gerald pulled out my package of Trojans and said, "This is Memphis!" He jerked up his hand and dashed the box to the ground. The remaining condoms, still sealed in foil, spilled out, and Mr. Gerald stomped upon them as he would a snake. Then, one by one, the elders turned their backs to me, as did Mrs. Earlene and Mr. Darnell, who forced a struggling Teena to do the same. I knew a general shaming ritual when I saw one, so I hurried before Mr. Gerald and tried to apologize. He turned away and I ran around him, knowing not to touch him but fearing if we kept this activity up we'd both get dizzy. Finally, I shouted, "I am sorry," which halted Mr. Gerald. He looked at me, arms crossed, as I yanked the blindfold from my neck and said, "Whatever needs to be done so I might stay and marry that young woman, that I shall do." I hoped my formal cadences might impress, but the sentiment was true: At that moment I would have done or given up anything to marry Teena, especially when it appeared she was about to be taken from me. Mr. Gerald moved closer. He smelled of the Borax they used to wash whites. At least thirty years older than I—perhaps more—he hadn't a wrinkle on his face until he smiled. "You would join us then? As an Assimilated?"

"As an Assimilated, yes," I said, nodding while I looked at Teena. Her parents' grips loosened, but they'd not let her go.

"Then there is but one thing," said Mr. Gerald, walking past me toward my cabin. At the time, I thought it curious no one else around me followed him directly. I know now none but Mr. Gerald understood what was about to commence. Still, all of us followed in a single line until we'd reached the door of my cabin, open from the earlier search for contraband.

"Enter," Mr. Gerald said, and I did, turning to look at Teena, whose face still shone with tears. I'd wronged her—I believed this—and wished for that first moment again in the woods, when her attempt at seduction was so natural and untainted. Pure as sex can be. But for now I had to perform whatever task Mr. Gerald assigned. And it was this: For a week I had to remain in my cabin, guarded by a rotating watch. In this time I was supposed to have no communication with anyone, no stimulation of any kind, intimate, physical or emotional, and above all, I was not allowed to travel to Memphis. "This cleansing has been undertaken by all who have by choice joined us," Mr. Gerald said, one hand on the door, the other pushing me inside. "When you emerge, then and only then will you be one of us for all your time on earth."

Before I could speak, he slammed shut the door. I thought I heard Teena call my name, but I might have imagined it.

I had known challenges before. Two weeks in an Arizona desert monastery, unable to say a word. Hiking through Inuit country, with only an aboriginal guide. Three hours on the Dallas outerbelt in August, trying to find the Denton exit. But the following week would prove to be the hardest challenge of my life. The privations—no books, conversation, little physical activity—were many and the cabin confining. Thank God I'd left the Trojans on my bed, making them easy for the elders to find, else they might have looked underneath and found my notes and pen. Not only might that discovery have lost me my chance at assimilating—which I so much wanted then—I wouldn't have had the items necessary to write the beginning of this particular account.

The ritual was understandable, as I could feel my interest in Two Box waning with each hour. When your prime interest is the sip of water you were promised six hours ago, suddenly a bottle of Miller and a bucket of

KFC fail to tantalize. And with the incentive that once I'd completed this onerous task I could marry Teena and make more members of the tribe, I endured every minute. My two meals a day weren't much—slightly better than bread and water—and as it had during my first week, my internal clock could not come to terms with my inactivity. I slept poorly, rising at midnight and failing to fall asleep for hours. For about two hours on my third day, my heart throbbed as if I'd been on the Stairmaster too long without eating beforehand. My hands tugged at my shaggy hair. I could not swallow away the constricting sensation in my throat. Yet this fit passed, soothed by a vision of Teena, amply pregnant, perhaps with twins. I could do this, I told myself. I would not be defeated.

Then the notes started to arrive and I knew I had to leave.

Because I was let out twice a day to urinate and/ or defecate in the woods (not at the lodge; I was to see none but my warders), I detected the guards' rotation rather early and saw that for at least four hours a day Joel tended to me, regularly after my evening meal. From the beginning, I whispered to him about basketball and once even mimed a jumpshot when we were behind the cabins. He remained stoic for at least five days until he said through clenched teeth, "They took our hoop away." An hour later, the first note arrived, and I was excited for the communication, though disheartened when I read it. "Teena says this is all a lie," it read. "J."

While I couldn't determine just what the note meant, and wished to learn the antecedent of "this," I wrote no reply, fearing it might be another test. I did not want to emerge in two days then discover I was not clean and had to start anew. The next note was, however, a bit more clear, arriving just before Joel's shift ended and Enos came on: "You don't have to be in there." I still didn't believe I had allies on the other side. In haste, I ate both notes—their pulpy surfaces difficult to soften—lest Mr. Gerald or another elder find them. I almost ate the paper on which I'd begun my account, but decided to hide it in my underwear instead.

A day later another note arrived, demanding reply but written in two hands, one which I knew to be Teena's though I'd never seen her handwriting before. "Don't do this for me," it read. Below, in the blocky lettering that appeared on the two before, Joel wrote: "What do you want to do?"

For a moment, I waited, reading and re-reading the note. Could it be a trick? Did the elders suspect I had a pen? I pulled mine out from my shoe. It was running low on ink, and I didn't have anything to draw blood, so I used the pen to tap on the door. When Joel responded with a tap of his own, I put my mouth to the bottom of the door and whispered, "I have a pen."

No time at all passed before he said, "Then write."

But what to say? I decided to test Joel first. I wrote: "What is the lie Teena spoke of? When I can send a note to her?"

I slipped it under the door and waited. When enough time passed for me to worry that Joel had taken it to Mr. Gerald, I knocked on the door with the heel of my foot. Joel tapped back and another note came through. The lie, of course, was this ritual of cleansing. All any other Assimilated had had to do was declare he wanted to stay and then go to work in Memphis for at least five years. Neither Joel nor Teena knew why Mr. Gerald had condemned me to this, though I suspected it was an attempt to break me, a brainwash to assure I stayed on, eager to earn a wage but unable to fashion an independent thought. Another paycheck: that's what the elders wanted of me, I determined, the rough board of my cabin floor scraping my bare skin. Soon, so soon, only the Collectors would sojourn to Memphis for the rent checks, then leave Mr. Clyde to determine how much to invest where. The days in Two Box would end.

But though I believed I'd discovered their racket, I didn't know what I was in a position to do. I wanted to leave. Of that I was sure. But how to proceed? With all those trips to and from the Compound, my blindfold kept me from knowing the way out. Remembering my uncle's odyssey, I didn't want to die trying to escape. I could try to endure the remaining day and then falsely proceed in the life of the Compound, but would my emergence end their surveillance? And might I be on the brink of some stress-induced collapse, one producing in me the meek attitude Mr. Gerald wanted? I had to act. But I needed help and turned to Joel, recalling the way he'd longingly looked at the dress shoes on his feet during the Choosing. Even though he'd taken them off, his last touch of them was as long as his first. This, along with the prohibition of his and Enos's makeshift basketball games, might assure I could get at least to the road and the gas station from which my uncle had phoned me. How long ago was that, I wondered, fearing my sense of time was more damaged than I knew.

Moving swiftly, I penned to Joel this: "Would you leave with me?" He didn't even write. "Yes," he said aloud. And while I wrote to ask him when, he said, "Let's do it now to catch them off guard."

Inside the cabin, I dressed like a fireman, made sure I had all my notes inside my underwear. In the lodge was my camera, several rolls of film, a compass, cooking stove, and watch—tools that had served me well on a number of expeditions and easily cost me a grand. Yet I was more than content to leave them behind. I made sure I had my wallet—the elders hadn't confiscated it—and, hands shaking, heat rising from my skin, realized there was one thing I couldn't leave without: Teena. I whispered to Joel to fetch her, but he said, "Can't. Someone'll see I'm gone and get suspicions."

"Try," I whispered. "Please."

After a long silence, I heard a heavy sigh and the slap of his bare feet against the hard ground. My throat clenched again, my dry eyes burned. Outside, it was probably in the twenties. The dry grass had been crunchy on my last trip to urinate. But my anxiety kept me warm. Sweating like an unskilled liar on the witness stand, I was unsure if we'd make it out, unsure what might happen if we were caught. Joel and Teena would be excused as youth, while I'd be viewed rightly as the one who had convinced them Two Box—with its opportunities, plenitude and most of all its variety—was preferable to the Compound. Right then, as I waited for Joel and wished for Teena, I knew how foolish I'd been, fantasizing so long for a place such as this. Out in the world, where I was often the only one, I would still have to face all the questions and attempts to get me to choose a side, but the same thing had been expected of me here, only with more rules and less pleasure. Whether I looked out and saw Teena with Joel or not, I knew I was leaving.

But after Joel tossed open the door, I saw standing next to him a sleepy Teena, clad in what looked like a gray sweatsuit. Still, she was heavenly. I moved to hug her. Joel dragged her away. "We've got to go now," he said.

"Go where?" Teena said.

"There," I said, pointing toward the lodge. Her heavy lids lifted and her eyes showed shock, though I couldn't tell if there was joy or fear in them. I reached for her as a door from one of the cabins creaked open. Joel and I bolted toward the lodge, though Teena slowed us down, pulling away and saying, "Where are you taking me?" in a voice that surely woke half of the Compound. More doors opened, and I saw Mr. Gerald, a nightcap flapping on his head and a nightshirt billowing around his legs. "No," he said, waving his hands above his head. "Stop them!"

More mulattos exited their cabins. There was one way out: the van. The keys would be, as they always were, on the hook outside the lodge's rear entrance. Surely, Joel, from all his hunting, know the way to the road that lead to Highway 61. Grabbing Teena's hand, we dashed toward the lodge, pulling her along. Mr. Gerald stepped in our path but Joel shouldered him out of the way, smiling savagely as though he'd wanted to do that for a long time. I snatched the key from the hook, opened the van, then we three raced past horrified faces and Mr. Gerald, on his knees, snatching his luminous night cap from his head and his face contorted into an endless no. Joel's directions were sure and certain and in no time at all we'd exited the Compound and were headed north on a two lane country road. I looked back to Teena and said, "I love you."

But she was asleep.

I almost stopped the van to wake her, but Joel called out, "She was doing what she was told."

"What?" I said,

"She was doing what she was told to do."

"Oh," I said. But there was nowhere to go but forward, so I plunged us deeper into the dark Arkansas night.

Before I dropped off Joel in Memphis and took out two hundred dollars from an ATM for his troubles, I learned my epiphany in the cabin was accurate. I'd been wanted by the elders as a Wage Earner all along and Teena had been instructed to keep me interested so I'd stay and add to their swelling coffers. Even her attempted seduction and eventual submission to me had been choreographed, as had all the times in between when she was kept from me. The affair with the Trojans had not been expected, but Mr. Gerald saw it as a way to assure I'd stay on the Compound, as my drifting attentions had been detected, and many were concerned I might depart, might expose them to the world. But Teena no more loved me than she loved Joel or Mr. Gerald. That was the hardest truth.

She lay in the van, still lovely, still asleep. I looked at her, wanting to smooth her hair from her eyes, then said to Joel, "Things do change. I can make her love me."

The sixteen-year-old seven-footer, who needed to buy a pair of shoes in the morning, stared at me as though I'd read aloud the sentiments of a Hallmark card. "Maybe," he said, looking away. Then, scratching one bare foot with the other, "Where do they play that game, hoops?"

"Find a building that says 'high school' and ask to see the coach," I said, handing him the money and a Memphis map. "You'll be fine." I paused, inhaled the city air, slick with motor oil and scented with diesel fumes. It tasted sublime. "I will make her love me," I said.

"Good luck," Joel said, turning then sprinting into the dark. As the echo of his footfalls diminished, I looked back at Teena, then drew near to inhale that sweet scent of hers. I had to get her away from here. Further, I had to throw off the mulattos, whom I was not about to underestimate. I drove us to the Amtrak station, and while she continued to sleep, I bought two tickets back to Urbana. At seven am we were on the City of New Orleans and headed to my home, my real home.

Two Box held Teena's interest for a time. After nineteen years of homemade soap, hand-me-downs with patches, communal meals and rigorous chores, who wouldn't find fascinating remote controls and Starbucks, cineplexes and Value Meals? But no matter what I bought, no matter what promises I made, I could not make Teena love me, or for that matter, my world. Once or twice, she let me kiss her, but I could feel the tension in her neck and shoulders and didn't try any more intimacies. We were both happy when we learned that Joel had found his way to Memphis East High and by the end of the summer he was ranked in the top fifty prep players and expected to command much attention from Division One schools. I hoped his good fortune—and a new pair of Nikes—might convince Teena to stay. But eventually, after hearing her sobbing many nights, I left a train ticket to Memphis on the counter and went to my office on campus. When I returned, I found my house cleaner than it had ever been, with nothing but the ticket missing, not even a note to say she had gone.

And so closes my account on the Wild Mulattos. When I resumed my writing from the preliminary notes I'd made in the cabin, I hoped I'd be cured of wanting to find Teena again, and now can say that my sole wish is she has been embraced by her people. But curiously, I also find myself in a position that Hans Zimmer must have been in when he pondered publishing his book. Certainly, no one will believe my strange tale. I have no evidence save for the scraps of handmade paper—and you can buy a reasonable facsimile in any stationery store. I'd never dare bother Joel or try to find any of the other mulattos who left. I'm sure they want to forget as much as they can of their former home. As for the remaining mulattos, knowing them as well as I do, I suspect they've moved to another location. Perhaps back to Louisiana or east to Florida or deeper south in Arkansas. Wherever they now reside, though, even were I to again stumble across their domain, I would not promote that discovery. I know too well where I belong.